"Did you check out the window to see who was at the door before you let me in?" Logan asked as he came into the house, pausing to secure the dead bolt again.

"No, I didn't think of that," she admitted.

"Well, you probably should," he said in a somber tone.

"Meaning?"

"Meaning that fire was definitely arson. And to be set that close to a house is different from the other arson fires I've investigated recently. Plus, the incendiary device was different, too." He studied her closely. "I think you're right to be concerned for your safety, Mallory."

Strangely enough, she didn't feel nearly as worried as she'd felt last night. Maybe it was the bright warm sunshine streaming into the house, or the fact she'd gotten some good sleep...or more likely it was Logan. Seeing him standing there in front of her, tall and strong and handsome, and being so protective of her...it was just what she needed.

Melody Carlson has worn many hats, from preschool teacher to political activist to senior editor. But most of all, she loves to write! She has published over two hundred books—with sales of over six million copies, and she has received the *RT Book Reviews* Lifetime Achievement Award. She and her husband have two grown sons and live in Sisters, Oregon, with their Labrador retriever, Audrey. They enjoy skiing, hiking and biking in the Cascade Mountains.

Books by Melody Carlson

Love Inspired Suspense

Perfect Alibi

PERFECT ALIBI

MELODY CARLSON

HARLEQUIN® LOVE INSPIRED® SUSPENSE

 LOVE INSPIRED BOOKS

Recycling programs
for this product may
not exist in your area.

ISBN-13: 978-0-373-44697-1

Perfect Alibi

Copyright © 2015 by Carlson Mgmt. Co., Inc.

www.Harlequin.com

Printed in U.S.A.

Be gracious to me, O God...
For my soul takes refuge in You;
And in the shadow of Your wings I will take refuge
Until destruction passes by.
−Psalms 57:1

To Christopher Carlson, my husband of 38 years
(and the only earthly man I'd completely trust with my life).

ONE

Mallory Myers loosened her death grip on the steering wheel. Taking in another deep, calming breath, she peered down the pitch-black road ahead. Even though her intellect told her that it was unlikely she was being followed, her instincts disagreed. In her mind's eye she could see Brock Dennison in his silver BMW, speeding down the highway, trying to catch her.

And yet, she knew this was preposterous. For one thing, Brock would barely be finished anchoring the eleven o'clock news by now, and she was two hours away from Portland. For another, he was Brock Dennison, the golden boy of the *Channel Six News*. Just the same, she checked her rearview mirror one last time as she slowed down to turn into her parents' darkened driveway. The headlights that had been tailing her were nowhere in sight now. Home safe.

Her parents' lodge-style home was nestled in the ponderosa woods, bordering the National Forest. Remote, yes, but a great place to lie low for a while. The perfect place to get her bearings and hopefully some sleep. Having a dad in law enforcement, with a well-stocked gun cabinet, added to her growing sense of security. *Home safe.*

She glanced over her shoulder as she hurried to the front door. Naturally, she could see nothing out there—and the tall ponderosa pines made the moonless summer night even blacker. The house was dark, too, but that wasn't unusual since her parents always went to bed with the chickens—even after they'd given up the henhouse. She turned her key in the front-door lock and quietly slipped inside, bracing herself for the familiar sounds of Barney's startled yips. Her parents' chocolate Lab was better than a security system. Nothing sneaked past him.

To her surprise the house remained silent when she entered, and she quickly discovered it was vacant. As she turned on the overhead light in her parents' bedroom, staring at the neatly made king-size bed, she remembered the message Mom had left earlier this week. Back before Mallory's life had fallen completely apart. Her parents were driving cross-country for a family reunion and wouldn't be home for two weeks.

Dad—her protector—was probably halfway across the country by now. That explained why he hadn't returned her call. Not wanting to upset her mother with her tearful voice, she'd left her disturbing message on Dad's work phone instead of on the landline's voice mail that her mother might listen to. But her parents were long gone and oblivious. And Mallory was more alone than ever.

Keeping the houselights low, she checked the doors and windows, making certain everything was locked tight. It was far more secure than her studio apartment back in Portland—a place she never wanted to go back to.

Her chest tightened at the memory of that horrifying scene in her bathroom last night. Mallory had made the gruesome discovery herself, yet still found it hard to believe. Her best friend, Kestra, had been murdered. Her throat slit, she was lifelessly sprawled across the checkerboard floor in a pool of shiny red blood. Mallory shuddered, feeling sick to her stomach as that macabre picture assaulted her again. Would she ever be free of that image?

It did no good to keep replaying it. It didn't help Mallory, and it was too late to help Kestra. *Poor Kestra!*

Still shaking from the chilling memory, Mallory hurried upstairs. First she went to her younger brother's old room, scavenging some of Austin's worn flannel pajama bottoms and a Blazers T-shirt, before hurrying across the hall to her childhood bedroom. But with no lock on the door, what was once a comforting space no longer felt completely safe. Nothing felt safe. Mallory scooted the heavy oak bureau in front of her door and reminded herself that no one knew her whereabouts. No one would come looking. Not yet, anyway. She needed to calm down. Just breathe...*breathe.*

After removing her rumpled work clothes—the same outfit she'd been wearing for two long days—she pulled on Austin's soft, worn clothes and climbed into bed. Then, with the silence of a dark mountain night enveloping her, she willed herself to let go, to surrender to some much needed sleep. But at 3:00 a.m., she was still wide-awake. Her heart was racing, her hands were still trembling— and her mind would not shut down. Despite the fact she hadn't slept the previous night, even after her friend Virginia forced her to take sleeping pills with warm milk, Mallory felt certain she would never sleep again. Insomnia had become her new best friend. And this stuffy bedroom wasn't helping.

Longing for some fresh pine-scented air, she decided to open the window. And really, her normally sensible mind pointed out, no one had followed her, and even if they had it was unlikely they would scale the wall to get into this room. That was ridiculous. But another part of her argued that she had just cause for serious paranoia—Kestra had been murdered. Not only had Mallory been the one to discover her best friend's body—in Mallory's apartment—but Mallory had received death threats, as well.

But replaying that scene was like this stale room—too

thick and heavy and hot for sleeping. Besides, common sense would have to prevail if she wanted to survive the madness that had invaded her life. She pushed open the window and leaned forward, breathing in the cool night air. And for a brief moment she almost felt like her old self again. Almost as if the past thirty-six hours of horror had simply been a nightmare. As if her dear friend had not been brutally murdered and Mallory was not in grave danger right now.

Mallory closed her eyes, inhaling deeply as she attempted to calm herself. She couldn't keep replaying this tragedy over and over. Not if she wanted to maintain some semblance of sanity. She sucked in a deep breath of night air and started to cough. Something was wrong. That sharp, acrid aroma wasn't the cool night-woods scent she'd known since childhood. *It was smoke!*

She leaned forward and sniffed again. There had to be a fire nearby. It smelled like wood smoke. A campfire, perhaps? Except that she knew there were no campgrounds in these parts. Plus it was mid-July—the height of forest-fire season. Open fires weren't allowed this time of year. And open burning was prohibited after sunset, no matter what time of year. She tried to think. Could someone be burning something in a fireplace or woodstove? On a hot day like this had been? She sniffed again. No, something was definitely wrong.

She narrowed her eyes, peering out her window into the inky darkness. Her window faced east, but it was too early for sunrise and she could see nothing. But the smell of smoke was getting stronger. Mallory pushed the bureau away from her door and raced downstairs. Running from room to room, she looked out all the windows, searching for the source of the smoke.

Out the kitchen window, she spotted a flickering light through the trees. An orange-ish glow that wasn't too far off. *A forest fire!* Her heart raced as she reached for the old wall phone by the breakfast bar. But the phone was dead. A cold wave of fear washed over her as she imagined a dark figure outside, armed with the knife he'd used to cut the phone line. Perhaps it was the same knife that had been used to murder her best friend.

She silently placed the receiver back in the cradle and bolted up the stairs for her cell phone. Was there a rational reason the phone was down? Was she overreacting? Perhaps it was related to the fire. Trying to calm herself, she knew the only way to survive this ordeal was to keep her wits about her.

She turned on her phone but remembered how the house's metal roof played havoc with her connectivity. She'd have to step outside to make a call. But what if the killer had followed her? What if he was lurking nearby, planning to kill her, just as she was certain he had killed Kestra only yesterday.

"Stop it!" she said aloud as she raced back down the stairs. "Just stop it!"

Despite her fear, she knew she had to make the 911 call. She couldn't allow her parents' home to go up in flames for some irrational fear. Bracing herself, she stepped outside and with trembling fingers pressed the numbers. Crouching down in the porch's shadows, she listened to the ringtone. Fortunately the dispatcher answered promptly, and Mallory blurted out her parents' address and news of the fire.

"It looks like it's about fifty yards west of the house— maybe closer." She peered toward the orange blur behind the ponderosa pine trees. "It's not real big yet, but it's definitely growing."

"Are you in any danger?"

"Uh, I'm not sure…" Mallory looked around, wondering if she might really be in danger—a different kind of danger. "I, uh, I don't think so."

"Are any structures involved in the fire?"

Mallory peered out toward the separate shop building where Dad kept his old Model A. "Not yet. But if the fire spreads, they will be."

"Can you stay on the line until assistance arrives?"

Mallory thought she heard something out in the woods, perhaps a spooked animal…or something more. "My phone's breaking up," she said as she opened the door. "It doesn't connect in the house, but I'm going inside—I think it's safer."

"Firefighters are on their way. The first responders should arrive in about ten minutes. Keep your eye on the fire and if you need to flee the house, call 911 again and give us your location. And if you need to—"

"Hurry!" Mallory yelled as she closed and locked the door. With trembling legs, she ran back upstairs, going into Austin's old bedroom since it faced west. There, she could observe the growing fire. Positioned in front of her brother's window, she watched the leaping flames. A forest fire in summer had always been one of her dad's worst fears about living next to the National Forest. And they'd had numerous evacuation alerts over the years, but she'd never seen anything this close before.

As she stared at the soaring flames, she felt certain this fire had been set by the same person who'd killed Kestra, the same person who had been threatening Mallory. And, although no one in the world believed her, Mallory felt sure that a certain charismatic newscaster from Portland's *Channel Six News* was involved. Somehow Brock Dennison had to be behind this. As irrational and unbelievable as it sounded, she just had a feeling.

Oh, she knew it made no sense. She also knew that the Portland police were convinced she was at the very least neurotic—and possibly something much worse. Even the *seemingly* sympathetic detective, Janice Doyle, had suggested it might even be the result of Mallory's sleep-deprived mind.

When Mallory had confessed her wild suspicions about Brock to them this morning, their expressions said it all. They clearly thought she was delusional. Detective Snyder hadn't bothered to hide his disbelief. When she'd shown them the words *You're Next* scrawled across her car's windshield, Detective Snyder had pointed out that lipstick seemed to suggest a woman had written it, and Janice Doyle had mentioned that the shade of lipstick seemed to match what Mallory had been wearing. She'd produced a tube of lip gloss to show them they were wrong, but they'd remained unconvinced.

She realized now how ridiculous she must've appeared to them. She'd brought all the notes she'd made during her sleepless night, pieces of information that seemed important, seemed to be pointing at Brock. They'd made so much sense to her. And yet as she'd laid them all out, going into all the details that had been bouncing around in her mind, the detectives had been unimpressed. They had politely listened to her and even recorded much of it, taking pages of notes.

But when it was all said and done they obviously thought she was making it all up. Probably just one more reason for them to suspect she was the murderer.

Detective Snyder had even insinuated as much. "Why are you going to much effort to point us toward Brock Dennison?" he asked as they were finishing up. "He has a perfect alibi. Cut and dried. He was on live TV when Kestra died."

Janice had placed a hand on Mallory's shoulder. "It's obvious you're exhausted. Take a break and think this all over. It's possible that your focus on Dennison is related to your breakup with him. Maybe you're not over it yet."

Mallory shook her head as she watched the fire outside.

She'd felt so convinced that Brock was behind everything—
now including this fire—but it really didn't make sense.
How would he even know she was here? She'd never
brought him to meet her parents—and this house was off
the beaten path. Besides that, why would he start a fire?
What would be the point?

She also knew from experience that most forest fires
were the result of lightning strikes, sometimes they flared
up from old strikes—possibly even a week old—that smol-
dered until the conditions were right and a breeze stirred
the embers up. Did she think Brock had sped over here
after doing the eleven o'clock news to light a forest fire—to
smoke her out? How would he even know her whereabouts?
It was just plain crazy. Maybe she *was* crazy.

Coming back to her senses, she realized that the fire was
moving steadily toward her dad's shop—the place where
he stored gas cans and propane tanks and lots of other in-
flammable stuff. Dad had always warned them that, in
the case of a fire, the shop would probably blow sky-high,
taking the house and everything with it. And based on the
usual mountain wind currents, the shop was in the line of
fire right now.

She couldn't just remain up here, watching it burn,
knowing that it would set the house aflame, as well. She
had to do something about it. Digging through Austin's
closet, she found his old letterman jacket and a Dodgers
cap. Pulling them on for protection against flying sparks,
she raced back downstairs and outside, locating the nearest hose. Her dad was well prepared and always kept long
sturdy hoses handy. Just in case.

Blocking out her fears and telling herself that help was
on the way, she turned on the faucet and stretched the
hose toward the spot fire that had popped up dangerously
near the shop, hoping that she could do damage control
until the firefighters came—whenever that would be. At

the very least, she hoped to keep Dad's shop from being engulfed. If that caught fire, the other structures would probably be goners, too. With the nozzle fully open, she positioned herself between the growing fire and the outbuildings. Her plan was to soak the ground and saturate the surrounding foliage, and hopefully keep the flames at bay until help arrived.

It felt like ages before she heard the sounds of sirens coming closer. Although she was relieved they'd finally made it, she was agitated that they'd taken so long. And with the fire even closer to the buildings, she wasn't about to stop her own firefighting efforts. Her single garden hose might not be enough to put out the whole forest fire, but until she was assured the firefighters were doing their job, she was determined to do her part. Besides, it was a distraction from her bigger problems.

It wasn't long until several sets of flashing lights appeared at the end of her parents' long driveway. Most of the vehicles parked upwind of the fire area, and a couple parked closer to the house. Soon there were people moving around and yelling back and forth.

Feeling that things were under control, Mallory was about to give up her post. But before she turned off her hose, she spied a new spot fire igniting some dry grass dangerously close to the shop. With hose still in hand, she dashed toward it, spraying the flames. But while she was running, she felt a heavy thud from behind, as if she was being tackled—and then she was pinned facedown on the muddy ground, a heavy figure on top of her.

With the wind knocked out of her, her heart pounded in fear. Certain it was the killer, about to put his knife to her throat, she tried to get enough breath to let out a scream, but all she could do was gasp for air—and pray for help!

TWO

Logan McDaniel had spotted the figure near the garage as soon as he'd come down the driveway. The youth was dressed in a letterman jacket and ball cap, and as soon as Logan approached, the kid took off running. Naturally, Logan chased him down, jumped him from behind and pinned him to the ground. Fortunately he was a lightweight and, despite the flailing arms and legs, it wasn't hard to keep the kid pinned down while Logan got out his flashlight. Hopefully he wouldn't have to use it as a weapon.

Using one arm, he flipped his captive over, shining the light straight into the kid's face. It wasn't a guy after all. It was a girl, and as the ball cap fell off, he could see that she had long dark hair.

"Help!" she screamed loudly, as if she thought he was some kind of an assailant. "Let me go! Help! *Help!"*

Still trying to get his bearings, he released her arms but kept her pinned down with the weight of his legs.

"Get off me!" She flailed at him. "Let me—"

"What are you doing here?" He moved side to side to dodge her blows. "You're a girl."

"Yes," she growled back. "Get off of me, you big lug!"

"First you better tell me what you're doing out here."

"I *live* here," she shouted angrily.

"No, you don't," he told her. "Deputy Myers and his—"

"The Myers are *my parents*! This is their house and I am—"

"Mallory?" As the realization hit him, he instantly eased back and, slowly standing, reached down to help her to her feet. "Is it really you?"

"Of course it's me. Who else would it be?" She wiped the mud away from her mouth, glaring at him with fury in her dark eyes.

"What are you doing out here?" He reached over to wipe a chunk of mud from her cheek, trying not to smile at how cute she looked. But she just shoved his hand away, scowling at him with suspicious eyes. She obviously didn't recognize him.

"Trying to put out this stupid fire," she spat.

"Did you start it?"

"Of course not!" She glared at him. "Are you nuts?"

"Did you make the 911 call?"

"Yes. Are you going to help put that thing out, or do you plan to just stand here yapping at me?" She pointed to an outbuilding. "My dad's shop could've blown sky high by now."

"My crew is on it," he assured her. "Don't worry. The fire's not too big. But good thing you called when you did. They'll have it under control soon."

She seemed to be studying him now, as if he looked familiar, but she wasn't really getting it. And he knew the yellow fire chief's helmet worn low on his head, plus the heavy clothes, made it hard to recognize him. Not to mention that their paths hadn't crossed in years. Although he wished they had. She leaned forward now, peering curiously at him. "Do I *know* you?" she finally asked.

"It's been a while, but yeah, you know me. At least you *used* to know me." He stuck out his hand to shake hers. "Logan McDaniel, at your service."

She blinked, then stared even harder at him. *"Logan?"*

"Yep." He glanced over his shoulder where several of the firefighters, some with hoses and some with shovels, were working their way toward them. "Looks like they're making good progress already. Probably have it contained before sunrise. Less than two acres I'd estimate. Small potatoes compared to last—"

"Well, it might be small, but it would've grown—"

"Hey, don't get me wrong, Mallory. Any fire is a serious fire. And I'm relieved it was small. And glad to jump on it early." He put a hand on her shoulder. "Sorry about tackling you like that."

She frowned at him. "Yeah, what's the deal? I thought firefighters were supposed to help people—not take them out."

"I'm really sorry." He pointed to the letterman jacket and the ball cap. "But dressed that way—I thought you were a teenage boy. I mean, there you are with a fire blazing nearby…" He held out his hands. "I approach you, and you take off running. What was I supposed to think?"

"I was running to put out that spot fire." She pointed to where the charred grass was still smoldering. Logan went over to stomp on it, crushing it out with his boot then dousing it liberally with a nearby garden hose.

"Well, I hope you accept my sincere apology, Mallory. We've had a serious problem with arsonists lately. Some tips have suggested they're teens. Last Saturday we had a human-caused fire that grew to nearly two hundred acres before our crew arrived."

"You really think kids set this fire, too?" She seemed to be studying him closely now. "I mean…you're certain it wasn't, uh, set by someone else?"

"What do you mean by *someone else*?" He peered curiously back at her. "Do you *know* something…?"

"No, of course not." She bit her bottom lip and glanced

away, as if she was sorry she'd said anything. Or as if she was holding something back.

"If you know something, you should tell me," he urged. "Mallory?" he persisted. "What's going on?"

He could tell by her face that something was wrong. Seriously wrong. Was it related to the fire? Did she have anything to do with it? As fire chief it was his job to investigate—and to be impartial. But he couldn't believe that Mallory Myers would have any sort of criminal involvement. Besides, this was her parents' home. Not that all family relationships were harmonious. "Do you know something about this fire?" he asked her again, using a firmer voice this time.

"Oh…no, I don't really know anything." It seemed as if she was trying to sound nonchalant. "I mean I just smelled smoke. I looked outside and saw flames and called 911. That's all."

Logan narrowed his eyes, studying her. Something about her story didn't ring true. And that bothered him. A lot. "Well, my guess is that this was a man-made fire," he told her. "We haven't had a lightning strike in a few weeks. And as far as I know, no strikes in these parts. Anyway, we'll know better when the sun comes up. Now, if you'll excuse me, I'll go give my crew a hand. I'd like to get this wrapped up as soon as possible. Just in case we get another call."

"Yeah, sure, of course." She nodded in what seemed like relief and, stepping back, she shoved her hands in the pockets of her jacket. She looked so sweet and vulnerable just now—dressed in those clothes with mud on her face, her dark hair glowing in the firelight. And yet she was acting so strangely…as if she were somehow involved in the fire. Logan felt confused…and conflicted. And those were not the sort of feelings that a fire chief, especially a relatively young one, liked to experience.

"You probably want to go in and clean yourself up," he told her in a brusque tone.

She looked down at her muddy clothes and nodded. "Yeah. Good idea."

As she walked toward the house, Logan just watched, dumbfounded. What was going on here? Why was Mallory at her parents' home when he knew they were on vacation? Why was she dressed like that? And what was she doing outside while there was what appeared to be an arsonist-set blaze going? What was going on?

Logan shook his head as he went to rejoin his crew. As happy as he was to see Mallory again—although he did regret tackling her—he felt torn. Something weird was going on here, and before this night was over, he was determined to get to the bottom of it.

"Doing some mud wrestling over there?" Winnie Halston teased him as she turned a shovelful of dirt over. Logan liked Winnie and appreciated that she worked as hard as any of the guys, but sometimes she got a little too friendly with him. It often felt like a tightrope walk to keep a professional distance, yet at the same time remain congenial and supportive as her boss. Sometimes he just wished she'd find another job.

Logan chuckled as he picked up a shovel. "Yeah, I guess it probably looked like that."

"Who was the kid you took down?" she asked as she shoved her spade into the soft soil. "And why isn't he in custody now?"

"The *kid* was a woman. Deputy Myers's daughter."

Winnie's brow creased with suspicion. "Do you think *she* set the fire?"

"According to her, she was simply trying to help extinguish it." He started to dig, helping to expand the fire line. He didn't really have to do the hard labor anymore, but it seemed to boost team morale to see him doing some of the grunge work alongside them. And since this was a small fire and not really in need of much managerial supervision, there was no reason not to help out. Besides, he felt guilty for ignoring Winnie a little too much this week. Such a fine line between sending a message and being just plain rude.

"So, what's this girl's name?" Winnie's voice had a twinge of jealousy.

"Mallory," he said in a flat tone.

"And you know for sure that she's really the Myers's daughter? I mean, isn't Deputy Myers on vacation? What's this chick doing out here all by herself while her daddy's gone? Sounds a little fishy, if you ask me."

"I know she's Deputy Myers's daughter because I went to school with her," he said wryly. "She was a couple years behind me."

"Fine. But how do you know she's *not* a suspect?" Winnie persisted. "This girl could be angry at her parents… maybe she gets even by torching their place while they're gone. Most violent crimes are committed by people known to the victims. Suspects are usually family or friends…"

"Been watching CSI again?"

"Just reruns." She smiled slyly. "A girl's gotta do something on a lonely night."

"Well, I'm relatively certain that Mallory Myers had nothing to do with this fire," he assured her. "As a matter of fact, she was the one to call 911, and when I tackled her she was actually just trying to hose down a spot fire to protect her dad's shop. Does that sound like a crazed arsonist to you?"

"You never know." She frowned. "What about that getup she had on? I saw her. Looked like she was trying to disguise herself as a kid. Maybe to make it appear this was part of the teen group you've been tracking. Suspicious."

He shrugged as he turned a shovelful of dirt over. He knew this was nonsense, but didn't want to argue the point.

"Maybe you're in the wrong line of work," he said. "Instead of being a firefighter, you should be working for the sheriff's department." He chuckled, but he wasn't really kidding. Everyone knew that Winnie loved putting her nose in everyone else's business.

"I'm just saying it's curious how this woman's out here by herself while her parents are off on vacation," she continued. "Just because you went to school with her doesn't mean she had nothing to do with this fire. And everyone knows we haven't had lightning in weeks. So you know it's gotta be human caused."

"Yes, I'm well aware of that, Winnie." He decided to insert some cool authority into his tone. Time for her to back off and focus on her work. Without engaging further, Logan set his shovel back in his truck then went over to give TJ a hand with unloading another hose from the water truck.

"What happened to that kid you stopped?" TJ asked as they maneuvered the hose toward the south side of the fire line, generously soaking the smoldering embers.

For the second time tonight Logan explained the little mix-up. But he didn't mind telling TJ. Besides the fact that TJ was his best friend, they'd gone to school together and Logan was pretty sure TJ would remember Mallory, too.

"No kidding? *That* was Mallory Myers?"

"Yep."

TJ laughed. "How'd she take that?"

"Pretty furious."

"Yeah, but as I recall Mallory was always a good sport." TJ chuckled.

"Hopefully she still is." Logan hefted the hose closer to the fire. The truth was, he'd always liked Mallory. More than once he'd considered asking her out. But something… or someone…always seemed to get in the way.

He wondered if that would still be the situation. Was Mallory in some kind of committed relationship? And even if she wasn't, what would be the point in pursuing her now? She lived in the city, he lived here. Besides that, something about her wasn't sitting right with him. The girl had troubles. He could almost smell it.

Logan worked with TJ for nearly an hour, but it was obvious that the fire was well under control and there was little need for Logan to remain on the line. Except that he was still mulling over some things.

"Is Mallory still good-looking?" TJ suddenly asked Logan.

"Kind of hard to tell with all that mud on her face." Logan chuckled as he leaned his shovel against a tree. No way was he going to tell TJ that she was even more beautiful now than he remembered her being back in high school.

"Never really told anyone, but I used to kind of have a thing for her," TJ admitted.

"Really?" Logan felt a small pang of jealous concern. "I never knew that."

"Well, I didn't go around advertising it." TJ grinned. "And you remember how shy I was in high school. Could barely speak to a girl." He punched Logan in the arm. "Not like you, Romeo. You always had girls hanging all over you." TJ nodded over to where Winnie was still shoveling. "Which reminds me. Winnie's been asking around about whether you're mad at her about something. Saw you two talking just now. Everything okay?"

Logan blew out a slow breath. "Yeah, sure."

"I know she rubs you the wrong way, but she's really not so bad. Once you get to know her better."

"I think *you're* the one who needs to get to know Winnie better," Logan teased.

TJ's grin faded and Logan waved a hand. "Better get your mind off the women and back on your work, TJ."

TJ gave him a mock salute. "Yeah, boss."

Logan saluted back as he informed TJ that he was going

to check the line. It wasn't that he was mad at TJ, but he didn't appreciate his friend's "helpful advice." It was clear that TJ was using Winnie as a smoke screen, probably a distraction from Mallory. Like TJ thought Logan was about to sweep Mallory off her feet. Although he had just *knocked* her off her feet. But seriously, neither of them would have a chance with Mallory Myers.

Besides having grown into her good looks, Mallory was a big-city girl now—a successful news writer for the *Channel Six News*, no less. Logan had heard Deputy Myers bragging about how his little girl had gone from being an intern to becoming the youngest journalist, at the age of twenty-three, for the prestigious Portland news show. And hadn't she been dating someone of influence, too? Clear signs she was out of their league.

As Logan walked, he considered his own limited history with Mallory. She'd been a year behind him in school, but he'd always thought she seemed like a sweet girl. Very pretty, with her shiny dark hair and big brown eyes. And smart, too. She was in his history class and outshone most of the seniors. Maybe that's why she'd caught his eye during his last year of high school. And during the following summer, when she coached his kid sister's lacrosse team, Logan went out of his way to be friendly to her every time he picked up Selma. But Mallory just blew him off. And Logan wasn't used to having a girl treat him like that. Eventually he'd just given up. It wasn't meant to be.

Ironically, he'd probably had his longest conversation with her tonight—after he'd tackled her. Maybe he needed to change his routine—some guys knocked 'em over with their charm, he could just knock them down. He chuckled as he kicked into a smoldering pile of dirt, pausing to give it some turns with his shovel. Not that he'd been looking for girlfriends much this past year. Getting appointed to chief had seemed to put the kibosh on his personal life.

But something about Mallory had really caught him off guard tonight. And it wasn't just because he felt guilty for knocking her down. No, there was something in her eyes that suggested all was not well. Something in her demeanor had reeled him in. So much so that he felt like stepping up to protect her. But protect her from what? The fire would be out before long, and he didn't really think her troubles were related to that anyway. At least, he hoped they weren't. Surely she wasn't an arsonist, as Winnie had suggested, here to sabotage her parents in their absence. That was just plain dumb. And yet he had to admit that Mallory's responses to his questions about the fire had sounded a bit like doubletalk. That wasn't good.

But it did give him a legitimate excuse to resume his conversation with her. After all, it was his job to collect information related to the fire, and his gut feeling had been that she was holding out on him. Something was troubling her. Unless he was mistaken, it was something pretty serious. And before he left this place, he wanted to get to the bottom of it.

THREE

As she took a quick shower—the first one she'd had since Kestra's murder—she couldn't keep her mind from replaying the events of the past few days. Would she always be haunted by fear? Mallory hurried to redress in the same work outfit she'd worn the past two days. It was what she used to call one of her "grown-up" ensembles, part of a limited wardrobe her mother had helped her to acquire when she'd gotten hired as an intern for the *Channel Six News*. "Dress for the job you want," Mom had wisely advised. Mallory had done so…and she'd eventually landed a fantastic job…but where had it gotten her?

She frowned at her pathetic reflection. A worn-out looking brunette in a rumpled linen suit and a pale green blouse that was anything but fresh. As she pinned her still-damp hair into a messy bun, she wondered why she'd told Mom to donate her old clothes to the resell shop last spring. Did she really think she'd never need her small-town wardrobe again? Plaid shirts and denim jackets were suddenly appealing. Comfortable and practical and much better than a bright orange jumpsuit. Not that she'd done anything criminal, although everyone seemed determined to pin something on her. Even when she'd told Detective Doyle she wanted to go home, she'd been warned not to leave the state.

Curious about the state of the fire, she went back outside to check. Although it was barely five, the western horizon was gray with morning light—and she still hadn't slept a wink. And felt pretty sure she couldn't sleep now. Or ever. A dozen or so firefighters were still at work and although there were various chimneys of smoldering smoke, no flames were visible. Mallory sat down in a front porch wicker rocker, staring down at a large metal pot of pale pink geraniums and trying to remember a time when life had been good. But nothing came to her. All she felt was a bone-deep sort of numbness.

She considered calling her dad. Chances were they'd reached Iowa by now—unless they were still on their way. But she had a feeling that if she heard his voice she would fall apart—and he would turn around and come back home again. Of course, that's what she wanted...but she knew it was selfish. Her parents rarely took real vacations, rarely traveled anywhere outside of the state. And as soon as they found out about all of this...first Kestra...then this fire... well, she knew that would be the end of their big trip.

Hearing footsteps, she looked up to see Logan McDaniel strolling purposefully toward her. To her surprise, her spirits lifted ever so slightly as she watched him approach. It was as if his mere presence breathed a spark of life back into her. Or maybe it was hope. Whatever the case, she was grateful.

It was interesting to see him by the light of day. Still as tall as she remembered from high school, he appeared a little more filled out now. Dressed in his firefighter gear, he looked ruggedly handsome, and his long slow stride suggested a steady sort of confidence. This man was comfortable in his own skin. While a part of her admired this trait, another part of her was disturbed by it. It was this same quality that had first drawn her to Brock and a frightened little voice inside her head warned her to watch out.

"It's a hundred percent contained," Logan announced as

he came up to the porch. Leaning against a post he peered down at her. "It should be completely out in a couple of hours."

"That's great news." She forced an uneasy smile. "Thanks."

"Just doing my job." He gave her a handsome grin, revealing even white teeth. "You clean up nicely."

"Thanks." She slowly stood, folding her arms in front of her.

"Are you okay?" he asked with a slight frown.

She bit her lip, unsure of how to respond. *Okay?* That was not how she would describe anything related to her life right now. Definitely Not Okay.

"I don't mean to intrude, Mallory, but you seem uneasy or upset, like something's bothering you. Need to talk?"

She felt a part of her softening. Why shouldn't she trust him? And yet…best to play it safe until she knew she could trust him. She sighed. "Well, witnessing your parents' home…about to go up in flames…that's a bit disturbing, don't you think?" She frowned then glanced away to avoid his eyes.

"Sure. It's understandable that you'd be upset over the fire."

"Plus I'm a little sleep deprived." She leaned back, wondering how much longer she could hold it together. His expression was so genuine…so sympathetic…it made her feel as if she was about to crack.

"I'm sure it's been a rough night for you."

"Try a rough couple days." She spoke sharply, then instantly regretted it. Besides not wanting to divulge too much, it wasn't as though it was his fault that her life was a train wreck.

His brows arched, and she could see the wheels turning in his head, but he kept his thoughts to himself.

"Sorry," she said quickly. "It's just that I've been, well, going through some stuff. Hard stuff. I came here to be with my parents—but I totally forgot they were going to be gone."

"Yeah, your dad's family reunion in Iowa," he said casually. "He told me about it just last week. He was really looking forward to the trip. Did you know that he hasn't seen all his siblings, all together in one place, for more than thirty years?"

Of course, this was upsetting to hear. For a couple of reasons. First of all, if she told her parents about everything—as she wanted to do—it would ruin their vacation. How selfish was that? But the other reason she felt bad was hearing how Dad had shared personal family information with Logan—instead of her. But maybe she'd been too busy. Too caught up in her own life. Too selfish.

"No, I didn't actually know that," she confessed. "But I do know that Dad has three brothers and two sisters. They live all over the country. I've met some of them, but I don't really know them very well. Not by more than just name." She studied Logan carefully. What sort of man was this? That her dad confided in him? Maybe she was mistaken not to trust him more.

"Can you imagine how it would feel not to see a sibling for that long—thirty years? I know I'd miss Selma a lot."

She sadly shook her head. "Truth is, I was just missing my own baby brother, but at least I got to see him last Christmas."

"How's Austin doing? I know he's still in the navy, over in the Persian Gulf the last I recall."

"That sounds about right." She stifled a yawn then regretted it. It wasn't that she was bored…just extremely tired.

He stood up straight. "Well, I can assure you that the fire is completely under control, Mallory. If you need to catch some winks, there's nothing to worry about now. You're safe."

She frowned toward the west where the sky was starting to glow like burnished gold. Nothing to worry about? She was safe? *Really?*

"I would like to ask you some questions about the fire," he continued in an authoritative tone. "Just to fill out my report. If you're too tired now, I can come by later. That is, if you're sticking around awhile." He looked slightly puzzled. "I mean, with your parents gone on vacation and all. You plan to stay here, anyway? By yourself?"

Before she could answer, she heard her phone buzzing inside the pocket of her linen jacket. Afraid it might be one of those nosy detectives again, demanding she return to the city, or maybe they wanted to lock her up…she wasn't sure she wanted to answer it in front of him. Just the same, she reluctantly slipped it out to peek. But seeing it was a text message from "unknown" made her curious. The last text she'd gotten from "unknown" had contained a veiled threat. And, although the police had not taken it seriously, she had.

"Excuse me a minute," she told Logan as she quickly read the words—shuddering at the meaning. This was no veiled threat. This was for real. With trembling knees, she sank back down into the wicker chair. As horrible as these words were, she read them again, letting the meaning sink into her.

You got lucky again. Ever see a burned corpse? Not pretty.

Someone definitely wanted her dead. She couldn't help but think it was Brock Dennison. Despite his rock-solid alibi, this nightmare seemed related to him. She'd witnessed his dark side while dating Brock. And she'd watched him lose it when she broke up with him six weeks ago. In her mind, Brock Dennison was capable of anything. Even murder.

"Are you okay, Mallory?" Logan moved closer, peering down with concern.

She nervously slipped her phone back into her pocket. "I, uh, I don't know."

"I really don't like to intrude, but I have to say something. I mean, it really feels like something's wrong. Want to talk about it?"

She glanced to the left and the right, searching through the trees in every direction, almost as if she expected to spy a killer hiding out there. Or even Brock, although she knew that was crazy. But someone had set that fire. Logan had insinuated that it was arson. And even if it wasn't Brock, someone had killed Kestra. And someone had threatened her. Was he out there now? Was he going to slit her throat the way he'd slit Kestra's?

Feeling completely overwhelmed and frightened to the core, she broke, beginning to cry. No, it wasn't just crying, it was sobbing—loud and uncontrollable sobbing. The next thing she knew, Logan had wrapped an arm around her shoulders and, helping her to her feet, he led her—practically carried her—back into the house.

When she regained her composure, or a semblance of it, she was seated on the old plaid couch in the living room, and Logan was sitting in her dad's leather recliner directly across from her. Leaning forward, he studied her with more than just casual curiosity.

"Wanna talk?" he asked gently.

"I—uh—I don't know," she told him. "It's kind of a mess and I really hate to involve you in it. I mean, well, it could be kind of dangerous."

He made a crooked smile. "Hey, I'm a firefighter, danger is kinda my thing."

She sniffed as she pulled out her phone again, trying to decide, but feeling too muddled to even think straight.

"Is this related to the fire?" His brow creased as he rubbed his chin.

She sighed. "I'm not sure. And, really, it makes no sense. Why would he…do *that*? But then again…there's the text message. And unknown caller ID? I mean, I'm sure it's from him. I mean someone I know…someone I don't trust…someone I consider to be my enemy—and it's pretty disturbing."

"May I see it?" Logan held out his hand in a way that suggested authority, but at the same time his eyes were full of empathy.

She pulled up the text, then handed her phone to Logan.

"'You got lucky again. Ever see a burned corpse? Not pretty.'" Logan looked alarmed. "What's that supposed to mean?"

"What do you think it means?"

"It sounds like a very serious threat."

"Yeah…" She looked down at the worn braided rug beneath her feet. The homely old rug had been here for as long as she could remember. Her great-grandmother had made it long before Mallory was born. For some reason, the even lines and predictable colors gave her a faint sense of comfort.

He handed her phone back. "Who sent you this?" he demanded.

"I'm not positive. But I honestly think it's my ex-boyfriend. Or someone connected to him. No one believes me, though."

"What kind of person is this?" He frowned. "I can't believe you ever had a boyfriend who would write something like that. Even if he is an ex."

"See." She held up her hands. "I told you that no one believes me."

"That's not what I meant." He looked frustrated. "I

mean, it's hard to believe a girl like you would be involved with someone who would send a text like that."

"Well, we're estranged now. *Very* estranged." She knew that was an understatement, but how much should she tell Logan? Could she really trust him? And would he even believe her? He already sounded doubtful.

"But, even if you are estranged…" He ran his hand through his messy hair. "To send something like that—I mean, it's a serious threat, Mallory. Whoever sent that is talking about someone getting burned to death. And we just put out an arson fire. Who do you really think sent this?"

"As you can see, it's from *unknown*." She looked at him with apprehension. Why was he being so persistent on this? Was it possible that Brock had already gotten to him? The way that Brock seemed to have infiltrated some of the Portland investigators? What if Logan was a part of Brock's deadly game? How many people did Brock control, anyway? Once again, it felt as if her head was spinning. Who could she trust? Anyone?

"I need to take a photo of it," Logan said suddenly.

She retrieved it from her pocket, pulled up the text and handed it to him, waiting as he examined it more closely and then, using his own phone, took a couple of shots. "So you honestly think your ex-boyfriend sent this?" He studied her closely as he held her phone out to her.

"I'm so tired that it's hard to think straight right now."

Logan stood up now, clearly agitated. "What's going on here, Mallory? You mentioned danger. And according to that text, you are definitely in some kind of danger. What kind of person is this? The guy who sent the text— *who is he*?"

"I'm not sure it matters… I mean, who he is or what he is…since no one believes me, anyway." She studied Logan closely. She wished she could trust him—she *wanted* to trust him. She needed someone trustworthy.

"Look, a fire was set outside your parents' home." He spoke slowly, almost as if speaking to a child. And perhaps she was being childish—maybe fear and exhaustion did that to a person. "You receive a text that refers to fire and death, a message that is clearly some kind of serious threat." He sat down on the couch next to her, staring intently into her face. "I'm not just asking you this as your friend, Mallory, although I'd like to think that we're friends, but I'm asking you this as the Clover fire chief, investigating an arson crime."

"Oh…." She nodded soberly. "Okay, then."

"Who sent the text?"

She took in a breath, sitting up straight, trying to think clearly. "I can't be certain, since it wasn't sent from his usual phone. But my guess is that it was sent by my ex-boyfriend. A guy named Brock Dennison."

"*Brock Dennison?* The anchor guy on the Portland news station?" Logan sounded shocked. "That's the guy you've been involved with?"

"How do you know that?" she demanded. "I mean that Brock and I are involved. I mean, we *used* to be involved."

"You just said it was from an ex-boyfriend."

"Oh…yeah."

"And you're saying that Brock Dennison is threatening you?"

She looked evenly into his eyes. "And you don't believe me, do you?"

Logan looked perplexed. "I didn't say that. I mean it's a lot to take in."

"No one believes me." She folded her arms in front of her, wishing she'd just kept her mouth shut. Why had she even trusted him?

"I'm sure that's because Brock Dennison is kind of a celebrity. A small-potato kind of celebrity. Not that I'm a fan." Logan frowned. "You won't catch me watching Portland news." He tipped his head to one side. "But you're seriously saying that Brock Dennison—the *Channel Six News* guy—sent that text to you?"

"That's right."

Logan shook his head with a perplexed expression. "Wow, that's a lot to absorb, Mallory. So do you think Brock Dennison has something to do with the fire, too?"

She felt a tiny glimmer of hope. Did he actually believe her? "I really don't know what to think. I have to admit it sounds unbelievable to think that Brock would do…well, the kinds of things I believe he's done…or is involved in."

"You make it sound like he's a serious criminal." Logan seemed genuinely concerned. "And if that text is from him, I'm inclined to agree."

"Really?" She felt strangely relieved that Logan looked worried. Maybe he wasn't in Brock's back pocket, after all.

"And you're obviously upset by it," he continued. "So I have to assume that it's not a joke or a romantic quarrel or—"

"There is no romance," she said quickly. "We only dated briefly. I broke it off a couple of months ago. The truth is, I can't stand him."

Logan slowly nodded. "So why would he send you that text? And why is he talking about fire?" He waved his hand. "Especially in light of what appears to be an arson incident." He narrowed his eyes. "Were you in communication with him earlier? I mean, about the forest fire?"

"No, of course not. He's the last person I want to talk to." She held up the phone. "Check my phone if you want. And, like I said, that text isn't from his cell phone. If it had been, I probably would've ignored it completely."

Logan's brow creased. "Then how do you know it's him?"

She frowned. "I just know."

"Okay, let's say it is from your ex," Logan said thoughtfully. "What do you think he's really trying to say? Does he want to see you burned? Was it a genuine threat?"

Mallory was still a little unsure of Logan but knew she had to trust someone. "I do believe it was a threat." She watched him carefully, gauging his reaction.

"A death threat to you?"

"I know it sounds a little crazy…especially when you don't know the whole story…but that's what I believe."

Logan looked uneasy or maybe confused. "So, let's be crystal clear. You're saying that Brock Dennison, your ex-boyfriend, probably sent you that text?" He pulled out a little notebook, flipping it open to write something. "About a burned corpse not being pretty?"

She simply nodded.

"And you're suggesting that the same Brock Dennison, the anchorman for *Channel Six*, has been *threatening* you, Mallory?"

"Look, this isn't easy," she told him. "And I feel like I'm stepping out on a limb every time I tell someone that I suspect Brock has threatened me. But it's true. I do believe he's involved. Even if this morning's text didn't come directly from him, I believe he's behind it. He started sending me a lot of veiled threats right after I broke up with him. Unfortunately, I didn't take them seriously. I just ignored them and dumped them."

He looked at his own phone. "Looks like it hit your phone at 4:27 this morning. About an hour after you called in the fire." Logan scribbled more notes. "Do you know Mr. Dennison's whereabouts right now?"

"Is this an official inquiry?" She knew she sounded defensive. Not for Brock's sake, of course, but simply to protect herself. All she needed was to get caught up in a false accusation in the small town of Clover—especially with her dad so far away. Never mind that no one in Portland took her other accusations against Brock seriously. But she knew that Brock had friends all over the place. In high places and in low. Brock Dennison was everybody's buddy. And he'd already threatened legal action against her if she "slandered" his name. He'd told her she could lose her job.

"That's right." Logan's mouth twisted to one side as he continued to write. "This is part of my investigation, Mallory. *Official.*"

"Do I need a lawyer?" Her question was part sarcasm and part sincere. One of her hopes in coming home was to get some advice from her dad's best friend, Al Brandt. Al was a decent guy and a respected attorney.

"Lawyer?" Logan frowned. "Why would you need that?"

Mallory rubbed her forehead and groaned. "I don't know. And, honestly, I don't know if I can do this, Logan. I mean, I haven't slept in a few days. My brain feels like oatmeal."

Logan looked sympathetic. "Okay, we won't try to do all of this right now. Just answer a couple of questions and I'll let you get some sleep. Okay?"

"Okay... I'll do my best."

"So, tell me the truth, Mallory, do you seriously think Brock had anything to do with that fire?"

"I wouldn't be surprised. Nothing about that man would surprise me."

"Do you think Brock would intentionally hurt you?"

Mallory stared at him. She was in too deep to stop. Besides he'd said this was an official investigation. Did she have any choice? "I think he would," she answered honestly.

"Okay..." He locked eyes with her. "Has Brock ever threatened to hurt you before?"

She took in a deep breath and made her decision. "He has sworn to kill me."

FOUR

Logan had a feeling he was in over his head. Not just with his personal feelings toward Mallory, but with this whole business regarding Brock Dennison, too. It wasn't as if he was a fan of the popular newscaster. Although some of his female firefighters seemed to be. Something about that meticulously groomed guy with the blond hair and flashy smile had always felt a little phony to him. And he found it hard to believe that Mallory had actually been involved with someone like that.

He also found it unbelievable that Brock Dennison had the nerve to threaten someone's life, much less commit arson, but he could tell by Mallory's face that it was true. Or, at the very least, she believed it was true. But facts were facts. There had been a fire, and Mallory had received a threatening text related to fire. Those two things were real enough. But getting the whole story, well, he didn't think it was going to be easy.

"So, Brock Dennison swore to kill you?" he repeated her words back to her, writing them down as he spoke. "Can you please elaborate?"

"The truth is he said it more than once. The first time he said it, he was really mad at me," she began slowly. "And although it caught me by surprise, I didn't take it too seriously. Or literally. You know how people say stupid things in the heat of the moment. I honestly didn't think he was going to kill me. I mean, Brock has a short fuse about some things. He can come across as a really nice guy, and then he'll turn on you."

"Right…so let's be clear. Do you think Brock is capable of violence?" Logan studied her closely. She looked so frail and tired, as if she were close to breaking. And yet she looked beautiful, too. He could tell that beneath all this, there was a quality of strength in her. "Mallory?" He reached out to gently squeeze her hand. "Is Brock capable of violence?"

"Yes," she quietly confessed. "He is. I know he is."

"Has he hurt you before?"

She simply nodded, staring down at her hands as if embarrassed. And maybe it was humiliating—telling someone she barely knew about the intimate details of a past relationship. A part of him felt slightly voyeuristic for pressing her like this. But for the most part, he just wanted to help her. How could he help her if she didn't tell him the truth? He wished she could just trust him.

"I know this isn't easy," he said gently. "But remember this is an investigation. And, really, you can trust me. But I can't help you if I don't know what's going on."

"Okay." She sighed. "Maybe I should start at the beginning."

"That would help a lot."

"I guess it started last winter…actually it was even sooner than that. Not our dating, but the relationship. For some reason, I caught Brock's eye early on in my internship. I can't even imagine why. I mean, other girls were constantly flirting with him. I never did. I was all about work. I took my internship seriously. I took newswriting seriously. I honestly don't understand why Brock went after me, but he did."

"I think I understand why." Logan sighed. "For starters,

you're a beautiful girl, Mallory. You're also very intelligent. And you have a sweet spirit. That's a rather attractive package, don't you think?"

She blinked in surprise, but said nothing.

"Seriously." He rubbed his chin. "Combine those qualities with the fact that you were focused on work—not flirting—well, that probably made you seem even more attractive. Kinda like playing hard to get."

"I wasn't playing—"

"I know. But you get what I'm saying. Some guys like the challenge."

She frowned. "I guess so. Anyway, Brock was intent on dating me. For nearly a year, I brushed him off. I didn't want anything to mess up my internship or my chances of getting hired. But he was relentless. Finally, after I was hired, I told him that I thought there were rules against dating in the workplace." She shrugged. "But Brock assured me that dating was acceptable. He pointed out others who were happily involved." She pushed a strand of dark hair away from her face. "Come to think of it, he even insinuated that dating him could *help* my position. But, honestly, that wasn't my motivation. And Brock is very persuasive and the truth is that, back then, I found him charming and attractive. And, even though I'd been pushing him away, I have to admit I was flattered by the attention. I finally gave in at Christmastime last year. I agreed to go on *one* date with him. You'd think I'd given him the moon."

Logan nodded. A real date with Mallory would feel like a gift to him, too. If it turned out that she was being honest with him. Somehow he felt she was. "So you started dating him about six or seven months ago?" he prodded.

"Well, we weren't really dating. It was *one* date. We went to a fund-raiser thing right after Christmas. Our next date—because he talked me into it—was on New Year's Eve." She paused to think. "We went out a few times after that, but we didn't really become a couple—well, not in my eyes, anyway—until Valentine's Day."

"Uh-huh?"

Mallory frowned. "Am I boring you? I mean, do you really need all this for your investigation?"

He shrugged. "Maybe…if it turns out that Brock really has something to do with the fire, it could be helpful."

She stared blankly across the room, as if trying to remember what she'd been saying. "Okay…so, anyway, I was totally honest with Brock right from the start. I told him that I was an old-fashioned girl and that I wanted to take things slowly. I figured that would turn him off because I knew he had a reputation for being a ladies' man. I thought it would send him running."

"But it didn't?"

"No. Looking back, I actually think he saw it as a challenge, like he could make me change."

"That makes sense." Logan tried to listen impartially, pretending not to be rankled by what he was hearing as she continued to talk about the early days of their dating relationship. It sounded as if Brock had done all the expected things—he gave her flowers and gifts, took her out regularly.

"But sometimes it seemed his attentions were as much for him as they were for me," she explained. "Sort of like he wanted to show off. Like it was always important that I would receive roses at work and he expected me to display them on my desk for a couple of days so that all the girls could see them. They would ooh and aah and act jealous." She clenched her fists in her lap. "What they didn't know was that Brock was becoming more and more controlling of me. He would tell me what to wear on a date. How to act and talk and walk. Like I was his little robot girlfriend. And if I questioned him, he would get irked. And the more we dated, the more intense it became. If I didn't comply, or if I questioned him, he could get really angry."

"Did he ever hit you?"

She pursed her lips. "Not exactly *hit* per se. But sometimes he would shove me really hard. You know, like up against a wall. I got a lump on the back of my head more than once. And if he was really angry, he'd pin me against a wall, shouting into my face."

"That's terrible. I can't believe you'd put up with that."

"Believe me, the first time he was abusive, I was ready to leave. But he was so apologetic and broken up over it the next day. He swore it would never happen again. I gave him a second chance and he kept his word...for a while."

"And then?"

"It started up again. After a couple of weeks, he lost his temper with me again. He told me he was stressed over work and that he was really sorry. And I stupidly rationalized that it was a one-time thing—even though it wasn't the first time." She shook her head. "But the next time it happened, there was no real excuse. And it felt even more intense than the others—and hateful. It was like someone pulled his trigger and he went off. Well, I guess *I* pulled his trigger. But the way he apologized afterwards, the way he brought me flowers and candy to work...well, it made me think this might be a pattern with him. Like maybe he'd done it before—in other relationships."

"Did you ask him about that?"

"I did. I'd done some research on domestic and dating violence for a news piece I was working on. And it was like reading about Brock. Like the writing was on the wall. When I confronted him with my findings and asked him about his past relationships, he got defensive and indignant. Somehow he made it look like I was the one with the problem. Like I had stepped over some line."

"But you still didn't dump the jerk?"

"I was seriously getting ready to, but based on what I'd read, I felt like I needed to do it carefully. I worked out this plan where I thought I was going to slowly cut him loose. Distancing myself, ignoring his calls. But he showed up at my apartment one night, demanding to know what was wrong. I admitted I was done, and he got enraged. He grabbed me and wrapped his hands around my neck like he was going to strangle me." She shuddered. "He told me he could kill me—he said it would be easy."

Logan felt a wave a shock run through him. "So you broke it off then?"

She nodded. "That was in late May."

"And how did he handle that?"

"He was furious. And for a while he was actually stalking me. He kept his eye on me at work. One time I caught him reading something on my computer. I'd spy him driving by my apartment complex occasionally. And he'd leave me lots of text messages, saying how much he loved me and telling me that I'd come back to him eventually. Really creepy. But at work he acted like he was the one to break it off with me, and he started a rumor that we were getting back together. It was weird."

"Yeah," Logan agreed. "Sounds weird to me, too."

"So…anyway… I've been apprehensive of him for quite a while. And then…well, just this week, I became downright fearful."

The sound of someone knocking on the front door made Mallory jump toward him, clutching Logan's arm with a look of real terror. But it seemed like such an extreme reaction that Logan wasn't sure it really matched what she'd just told him. Certainly she should be worried about being threatened by someone. But this fear seemed deeper, so much so that Logan wondered if she had told him everything.

"It's just TJ," he assured her as he looked out the window. "One of my firefighters." He hurried to open the door.

"Something out here you should see, Chief." TJ jerked his thumb over a shoulder. "We think we found the cause of the fire."

"Human?"

"Oh, yeah."

"I'll be out in a couple minutes." Logan returned to where Mallory was still huddled in a corner of the couch and, placing a comforting hand on her shoulder, he peered intently into her eyes. "I know you've been through some sort of serious ordeal, Mallory. And I want to hear the *whole* story, but I really think you need to get some rest first. Are you going to be okay here? Or do you want to go to town and—"

"I'll be fine here," she assured him.

Logan was uncertain.

"Go ahead, find out about the fire stuff," she told him. "Really, I'll be okay."

"Maybe so. But I think I'll just stick around the place while you're resting."

"You don't need to do that." But even as she said this, her eyes said something different. Her eyes seemed to be pleading with him to stay. And that's what he intended to do.

"It'll take a while for me to complete my investigation," he assured her. "Long enough for you to have a good long nap. At least a few hours. And by then I'll have more questions for you." He held up his cell phone. "Let's exchange numbers. Just in case you need to call me while I'm out there poking around."

"Okay…" As she recited the numbers, her voice sounded groggy. Hopefully she'd be able to get some sleep now. He could tell she needed it.

"I'll be outside, walking around the property, looking for additional clues and taking some photos, but I can be back in here within minutes if you need me." He peered into her half-open eyes. "Okay?"

"Thanks, I appreciate it." She leaned back into the couch as if she was about to nod off.

"I need you to lock the doors after I go outside," he explained.

She nodded with a look of realization. "Of course. Thank you."

He led her to the front door and, after he exited, listened as she clicked the dead bolt into place. He wasn't certain that she needed to take such precautionary measures, but at the same time he wasn't certain that she didn't. And if the rest of the evidence supported his suspicion of arson, it really did make this place a crime scene. In that case, he couldn't be too careful. In fact, it was possible that the criminal was still nearby. Logan wished he'd brought his gun. Because he suddenly felt more than just a little protective of this woman. There was no way that Brock Dennison—or anyone—was going to hurt her. If they did, they'd have to go through him first.

FIVE

It was almost noon when Mallory woke up. It took her a moment to realize where she was—and even then she couldn't remember why she was sleeping in her parents' king-size bed. But then it hit her... Kestra's murder... fleeing to here for safety. For some reason that all seemed further away now. Perhaps it was from getting some sleep or from the cheerful sunshine pouring through the big slider window. It was very comforting and almost made her feel safe. Remembering that Logan was still here added to her a sense of security. At least, she hoped he was still here. It had been hours.

As she went into the living room, she felt a rush of fear—what if Brock was here, too? What if he really was the one who'd set the fire? Or, even worse, what if he'd hurt Logan while she was sleeping? Her heart began pounding with fear as she peered out the window. The Clover Fire Chief pickup was still parked in the driveway, which meant Logan hadn't left. But where was he?

With some trepidation, she stepped outside onto the front porch and glanced around, hoping to spot Logan. But he was nowhere in sight and, despite the warm sunshine, a chill ran through her. What if Brock was here? What if he'd found Logan? She hated to imagine what Brock might do if he knew that Logan was helping her. With trembling hands she pulled out her phone and located Logan's number. As she listened to it ring, she wondered what she'd do if something had happened to him. In just a few short hours Logan McDaniel had become very dear to her. Despite her paranoia, she trusted him now. Even more reason for Brock to hate him.

She heard the crunching of underbrush and turned to peer into the tall ponderosa pine trees, squinting through the shadows and light, trying to see what had made that noise. She knew it could be an animal, but her instincts reminded her that it could be human, too.

"Answer the phone," she whispered frantically as she moved closer to the front door.

To her relief, Logan answered with a cheerful "Hello."

"Oh, I'm so glad you're okay," she said suddenly.

"Why wouldn't I be?"

"I don't know." She glanced over to where she'd heard the noise, trying to slow down her pounding heart. "Anyway, I'm awake now," she said nervously. "I know you wanted to finish questioning me about the fire…and stuff."

"Great," he told her. "I'll be back there in a few minutes."

After she said goodbye, she hurried back inside, locking the door again. She knew she was probably overreacting. Or maybe not. Would she ever stop second-guessing her every move? To distract herself, she focused her thoughts on Logan and suddenly decided that she wanted to put her best foot forward. Grabbing up her purse, she hurried into the master bathroom and peered into the brightly lit mirror. There probably wasn't much she could do about the strained look on her face or the shadows beneath her eyes, but she made sure she didn't have drool marks on her chin before she applied some lip gloss and mascara. She was just finishing when she heard a loud knocking on the front door. The sound made her jump, but reminding herself it was Logan, she hurried to let him in.

"Did you check out the window to see who was at the door before you unlocked it?" Logan paused to secure the dead bolt after he closed the door.

"No, I didn't think of that," she admitted.

"Well, you probably should," he said in a somber tone.

"Meaning?" She studied him closely, wondering if—like her—he was becoming aware of the potential danger.

"Meaning that fire was definitely arson. And it's different from the other arson fires I've investigated recently. None were set this close to a house. Plus the incendiary device doesn't match." His expression was very serious. "I think you're right to be concerned for your safety, Mallory."

Strangely enough, she didn't feel nearly as worried as she'd felt before. Maybe it was because he seemed concerned, or simply because he was here with her. It was easy to be frightened when she was alone in the dark of night. But somehow, with the sun shining and seeing Logan in front of her, tall and strong and handsome, and acting so protective of her…it changed things. It was just what she needed. Well, that and some food. Her stomach rumbled loudly as if to confirm this.

"You hungry?" He pointed to her midsection.

She gave him a sheepish smile. "I guess so. I honestly can't remember the last time I ate. I think it was yesterday morning…a stale donut."

"That's not good." He grimaced. "I'm getting hungry, too."

"I wish I could offer you something here, but my efficient mother cleaned out her fridge before they left. Although there's always the pantry. There's always something in there. Soup or—"

"Let's get out of here," he said suddenly. "Let's go to town. Let me take you to lunch, Mallory."

Even though this hadn't been her original plan—she'd

wanted to lie low for the whole weekend—she couldn't say no to him. To be fair, she'd probably agree to almost anything he suggested. Something about this guy—maybe it was his eyes, maybe it was his smile, maybe it was his fire chief badge—made her feel safe with him.

Logan suggested she ride with him and, once again, she agreed. "Will you run the siren?" she teased as he opened the passenger door for her.

He laughed. "I can if you want."

She waved her hand. "That's okay. No need to draw unnecessary attention."

As he drove to town, he asked her some rather general questions about Brock. She could tell by his tone that he was having difficulty believing that the popular *Channel Six* newscaster would have sneaked over here and ignited a forest fire. And who could blame him? In the light of a warm summer's day, it sounded preposterous—even to her.

Even so, he did appear convinced that something was seriously amiss. "It doesn't seem like a coincidence to me," he said as they came into town, "that you received that threat shortly after the fire was set. I'm not sure what's going on, Mallory, but I'd like to get to the bottom of it. In the meantime, I'm not sure that it's safe for you to be at your parents' house. Do you have anyone in town you can stay with?"

She considered this. "I can't think of anyone offhand…" She suddenly remembered the break-in at her apartment… the image of Kestra on the bathroom floor…and all feelings of safety evaporated. "I'm not sure I like the idea of staying with someone…putting them in danger, too." Her earlier hopefulness seeped away, replaced with apprehension and fear.

"You okay?" he asked as he turned onto Main Street.

"Uh, yeah…just thinking."

"About Brock?"

"Sort of." Mallory felt uneasy at the realization that she

still hadn't told Logan about what happened to Kestra. How did one begin to tell something so horrendous? Even talking to the detectives yesterday had been difficult. As devastated as she was for Kestra, Mallory wished there were a way to just purge the whole thing from her mind. The last thing she wanted to do was talk about it to Logan—to confess that she was considered a suspect. But he needed to hear the whole story. It was only fair.

"You mentioned that you, uh, you don't watch the Portland news much," she said carefully as he pulled up to The Lone Pine Diner. "But you probably have some news sources, right? You read it online...or in the newspaper?"

"Sure." He waited as a car exited a space in front of the restaurant. "It's not like I live under a stone." He chuckled as he pulled into the space. "Well, some people might think I do. But, yeah, I try to keep up. Although I've been pretty absorbed with these arson investigations this week. I'm probably behind on current events."

"Yeah...right..." She took in a deep breath as she reached for her purse. "So have you heard about the young woman who was brutally murdered in Portland just two days ago? Wednesday night..." She could hear the flat tone in her voice—emotionless and dead.

"Not that I can recall." He gave her a slightly puzzled look. "Why?"

She twisted her purse handle. "Well, maybe I should tell you about it."

He frowned as he removed the key from the ignition. "Okay, but let's go in and get something to eat."

"Definitely," she declared with relief. "You're right. We need food."

"Yeah. Never discuss murder on an empty stomach... right?" He gave her a lopsided smile.

As they walked into the restaurant, Mallory called on all her self-control to push every thought of Kestra's grisly murder from her mind. Right now she needed to focus on getting some nourishment. Something she hadn't had for days. And without the basics like food and sleep, she would be useless, anyway. At least she was safe right now. In a public place. Logan by her side. It seemed unlikely that anything could go wrong. As they entered the diner, a county deputy at the counter exchanged greetings with Logan. *See?* she asked herself. *How much safer can it get?*

After they were seated at a corner table, Logan grew somber. "I know we have a lot of serious talking to do," he began, "but while we're eating, let's just keep it light, okay? Better for digestion."

She nodded eagerly. "Absolutely."

He looked relieved. "And we can use this time to get re-acquainted. I want to hear about your job in Portland and why you were able to give up our sweet little town of Clover to live in the big bad city." He grinned as he picked up a menu. "All right, that's not fair. I know lots of folks who would choose city living over this. It's just that I happen to like it here."

"There's a lot to like," she admitted. And right now it was more appealing than ever. The thought of returning to Portland…to her apartment…her job…it sounded as daunting as climbing Mount Everest.

"So tell me about your career." Logan laid his menu down, listening intently as Mallory told him about taking journalism in college. "I'd always dreamed of working on a TV news show, but everyone acted like it was the impossible dream."

Mallory paused as a pretty young waitress named Corkie took their order. She didn't recognize her, but Corkie was obviously on friendly terms with Logan. And why not? But, unless it was Mallory's imagination, Corkie was being pretty chilly to her. Not to mention staring rudely. Maybe it was Mallory's rumpled-looking suit. Whatever the case, Mallory was glad when Corkie finally left.

Mallory continued to tell Logan about her job, moving from college to her internship at the television station. "It was so amazing to get it. Especially since it seemed like half of the journalism students had applied for it. Mom told me I landed it because all her church friends had been praying for me. And then, after just one year, they took me on as a full-time staff writer. The youngest one they'd ever hired." She smiled to remember how good that had felt. But then her smile faded when she remembered what Brock had told her...after she'd broken it off with him.

"What's wrong?" Logan asked.

"Oh, nothing." It wasn't so much that she wanted to keep it from him, but as he'd suggested, they should eat this meal in peace. She took a slow sip of water, trying to erase Brock's vengeful words from her mind. *You only got this job because I put in a good word for you,* he'd told her. *Without me, you're nothing. You'll see.*

Mallory forced a smile. "Enough about me. I want to hear about your career. I know you're the fire chief and, according to my dad, you're the youngest chief Clover has ever had." She held up her water glass in a toast. "Here's to you and me having something in common."

He clicked her glass with twinkling eyes. "Here's to having a whole lot more in common."

She felt her cheeks warm but hoped that his words would come true—that they would get better acquainted and then...who knew?

He told her about attending college while volunteering as a firefighter, and how he'd felt lucky to get a job in his hometown. "I don't know if you heard, but my dad died while I was in college. I wanted to be around to help my mom and sis."

"I'm so sorry about your dad," she told him. "I hadn't heard. That's so great you can be here for your family."

They continued to visit until their lunch was served. Fortunately the diner was busier now and Corkie didn't loiter long, but she did give Mallory a slightly glowering look. Was it possible that she was jealous? That seemed silly. And silly to fret over it. Especially since, for the first time since Wednesday night, Mallory felt ravenous. As they ate their food, they continued to chat congenially. Almost as if this was a date. And Mallory felt like a normal person. Almost, anyway. But it did give her hope.

"Logan!" A redheaded woman in a dark blue uniform came up to their table with a big smile on her face and a newspaper in her hand. "I was just looking for you."

"Oh." Logan's smile looked stiff. "I stayed on to investigate at the Myers' place. I'm on my lunch now."

"I can *see* that." The woman stared at Mallory with a creased brow.

Logan looked at Mallory. "This is Winnie Halston," he said politely. "She's one of my firefighters." He looked back up at Winnie. "And this is Mallory Myers. She's Deputy Myers' daughter and—"

"Oh, I know *exactly* who she is." Winnie waved her newspaper. "In fact, she's on the front page of this morning's news*paper*." She pointed to a photo of Mallory, next to a photo of Kestra.

"What's that about?" Logan looked understandably confused.

"You didn't know that Mallory is a suspect in a pretty gruesome murder case?" Winnie's auburn brows arched high.

"What?" Logan looked from Winnie to Mallory.

"You weren't aware that you're having lunch with a murderer, Logan?" Winnie laughed, nudging Mallory in the arm with her elbow. "Oh, I'm sure you're innocent, honey.

I mean the police wouldn't have let you out if you were guilty, would they? But, hey, you're on the front page. Must be thrilling."

"Not really," Mallory said in a flat tone. "In fact, Kestra was my best friend and I've been—"

"I know!" Winnie waved her newspaper. "Says here that you and the murder victim were in a love triangle with *Brock Dennison.*" She turned to Logan with wide eyes. "You know who *that* is, don't you? Just the hunkiest news guy in the Northwest. I watch him every chance I get. At six and eleven. *Brock Dennison.*" She said his name dreamily. "No wonder he's got girls fighting over him." She laughed.

"What on earth are you saying?" Logan demanded.

"Oh, it's all right here." She dropped the newspaper on his empty plate. "Hear ye, hear ye, read all about it."

"Just because it's in the paper doesn't mean it's true," Mallory said in a wooden tone. She felt her stomach turning as she clenched her fists beneath the table. "News writers don't *always* get their facts straight." She looked at Logan. His eyes were locked on the newspaper and his expression was grim as he stared at the article on the front page.

"Maybe so," Winnie said back to her. "But you know what they say…where there's smoke, there's fire."

"What's that supposed to mean?" Mallory demanded.

"It means I think it's a little suspicious that a murder suspect shows up here while her parents are gone and suddenly their house nearly burns down."

"What?" Mallory glanced over at Logan, but he was still intent on the newspaper.

"Strange coincidence, don't you think?"

"I honestly don't know what to think," Mallory said in all sincerity. "But I'm pretty sure that the same person who killed my friend is responsible for the fire, too."

"Yep." Winnie gave a victorious nod. "Just what I am saying."

"Huh?" Mallory felt slightly dazed now.

"Sorry if I interrupted your lunch." Winnie patted her on the back. "But I just thought it was pretty exciting to think that a murderer—from our own little town—has been dating Brock Dennison. And to be a murder suspect and possible arsonist, well, it just has the makings for a real good Lifetime movie." She nudged Logan. "Don'tcha think?"

Logan just rolled his eyes. "I *think* you've made your point, Winnie. Now if you'll excuse us."

"You coming back to the station?" she asked as she moved away from their table.

"Yeah. My shift is over at three. I'll be back before that to do my reports." As he stood, he pulled out his wallet and tossed a twenty down. "Come on." He reached for Mallory's hand. "Let's get outta here."

Leaving the detestable newspaper on the table, he led her toward the door, but before they could exit, Corkie came out and spoke to Logan in a low voice. "I heard what Winnie just said," she said. "I thought that was who you were with, but I didn't want to be rude and say so."

"Gotta go," he said abruptly.

"You be careful," Corkie called out.

"Always am," Logan called back as he opened the door.

Mallory felt her stomach churning as they went outside into the hot sun. She hoped she wasn't going to throw up again. She'd done enough of that on Wednesday night. Logan was still holding her hand as he led her to the pickup. He said nothing as he opened the passenger door and helped her in. His gestures were polite, but his expression was grim. Mallory knew she had some explaining to do.

SIX

Logan wasn't normally speechless, but the scene in the diner had left him feeling somewhat blindsided. Not to mention furious. What in the world was going on here? He glanced at Mallory as he started his engine. How was it possible that this sweet and slightly helpless girl—the one he wanted to take in his arms and protect—was a murder suspect? *How could that be?*

But instead of reacting in anger, he knew from experience that it was better to wait. Count to ten…or a hundred, if necessary. It was one of the traits that had probably helped him to earn the position as fire chief. As he turned off Main Street, he considered this factor—how did it look for the Clover fire chief to be consorting with a murder suspect? Not that he wanted concerns for his image to control his life. But he did have a certain responsibility.

"I want to explain," Mallory said quietly. "Everything. If you're willing to listen, that is."

"Of course, I'm willing to listen," he said in a slightly sharp tone. "I just wish you would have told me sooner."

"I wanted to tell you about it before lunch," she said slowly. "Remember, I tried to broach the subject? But you said we shouldn't discuss murder on an empty stomach."

"Right…but I had no idea we were talking about a murder where you're the suspect." He headed for the city park, which was fairly void of visitors today. Probably due to the afternoon heat. He found a somewhat secluded spot in which to park, but as he walked around to open her door, he felt torn. Was he being a complete fool to further this relationship? The smart thing might be to take this girl back to her parents' house and forget all about her. Or maybe his gut was right—maybe Mallory truly was an innocent small-town girl who'd gotten caught up with something foul… and was in need of his help. As he gave her a hand to get down from the truck, he sincerely hoped it was the latter.

"I'm so sorry I didn't tell you all this before," Mallory said as they sat down on a shady park bench. She looked at him with tear-filled brown eyes. "I tried to think of a way to explain it this morning, when I was telling you about Brock…but it's just so complicated. I didn't want you to think less of me, and I couldn't think straight."

"I can understand that." He spoke slowly, trying to appear more patient than he felt. "How about you tell me now. Just start at the beginning, okay? I need you to tell me everything. And just remember that this conversation is part of the ongoing arson investigation. I need all the facts." He pulled out his notebook and waited.

"The beginning…? Well, I told you about my relationship with Brock Dennison, the beloved TV anchor, the golden boy, everyone's best buddy. And how he handled it when I broke it off with him. What I didn't tell you was that Brock started dating my best friend, Kestra, a few weeks ago."

"The murder victim."

"That's right." She extracted a tissue from her purse, using it to blot her tears. Part of him wanted to take her in his arms and comfort her, but another part was holding her at arm's length. Why had she kept this from him?

After a long lapse of silence, Logan's patience was wearing thin. "So what about this murder, Mallory? Tell me what happened to your friend? I want to hear about the love triangle." He grimaced as he said this. "Please, explain that, if you don't mind."

"I don't know where to begin."

"How about at the beginning."

"Okay." Mallory's brow creased as she took in a deep breath. "Kestra was my best friend. We were roommates during the last couple years in college. In fact, she shared my studio during the year of my internship. But then she got her own place over on the west side. But she still came over a lot. And I let her keep a key. And because my apartment was closer to her work, she sometimes came there to change her clothes for a date or whatever."

"But the love triangle?" Logan knew he was pushing, but he also knew he needed to get back to the station before his shift ended. "What was up with that?"

"First of all, there was no love triangle. That is just journalistic hyperbole. I was completely done with Brock. I knew it. He knew it. Kestra knew it. But Brock went after Kestra about a month ago. And, even though she knew he was a jerk, Kestra was just blown away by his attention. She couldn't believe that Brock Dennison wanted to date her. She called me to ask if it was okay, and I went ballistic. Not because I cared about Brock. *Because I cared about Kestra*." She clenched her fists. "I knew something was fishy—I actually thought Brock was using her to get to me. But worse than that…I was afraid she'd get hurt."

"And she did get hurt. Murdered." He studied her closely, gauging her reaction.

"That's not what I meant. I was worried she'd get her heart broken." Mallory's face seemed to pale and her hands began to tremble. "And maybe I was worried she'd get physically hurt, too. But I never imagined she'd be killed. And Brock's threats to kill me—at least I assumed they came from him—weren't until later. After he and Kestra were dating."

"But you believe her death is related to Brock?"

"I do."

"Just tell me what happened," he said quietly.

"Kestra was murdered in my studio apartment on Wednesday night." She paused as if trying to get her bearings. "Just two nights ago I came home from work. I'd seen her car parked down below so I wasn't even that surprised when the apartment door wasn't locked. I called out for her as I put a small bag of groceries in the kitchen. When she didn't answer, I assumed she was in the bathroom.

"That wasn't unusual. But I didn't hear the shower or anything, so I tapped on the door. It was partially opened. When she still didn't answer, I pushed it open and there she was, partially dressed and lying in a pool of blood on my bathroom floor." Tears began falling down her cheeks. "Someone had—had slit her throat. Her eyes were still open. So I knelt down in the blood. I—I picked up her wrist to feel for a pulse. Nothing. She was dead. It was so horrible. Blood was everywhere...even on me after I checked her. And on my phone when I called 911.

"I—I went into shock while I waited for help to arrive. I'd never seen anything like that in my life. It was so horrifyingly gruesome! I feel sick every time I think of it. But I can't help but think of it." She crumpled into sobs and Logan took her in his arms, trying to comfort her.

"I'm sorry to make you talk about it," he said quietly. "But I need to hear your side of the story. I need to hear the truth."

And so she continued to tell him about the police arriving, and how she was taken in for initial questioning that night. "The police told me they needed my help to find the murderer. And I believed them. I answered all their questions and told them everything I knew. Everything I could think of. Then I spent the night at a friend's house. But I couldn't sleep. I'm sure I was still in shock. And I kept running everything through my head and by morning it seemed to be clear. And there was a death threat on my car windshield. Threatening messages on my phone. Like that one this morning. I knew that somehow Brock was involved. He had to be. It was the only thing that made sense. So I called the detective and told her that I had more information and that I wanted to help them to get her killer."

"Brock."

"Well, I knew that it couldn't be Brock by himself. I wasn't stupid. Everyone knew that he'd been on live TV when Kestra was killed. A rock-solid alibi. But I still knew he had to be involved. So I went in to tell Janice Doyle. She's a detective I thought I could trust. I told her all about Brock."

"And did she believe you?"

"At first I thought she did, but then Detective Snyder started questioning me pretty intensely. He seemed to have come to his own conclusions…mainly that I was involved in the murder. He suggested it was a crime of passion—a jealous girlfriend getting even. All kinds of crazy pieces he'd been gluing together. It got really intense and I'm sure I said some pretty stupid things."

She sighed. "I was tired and frustrated. And angry that they wouldn't believe me. That they actually thought I could have murdered my best friend and was trying to implicate Brock! It was totally ridiculous and backward… and yet they were serious. I honestly felt like the whole world was going nuts. No one seemed to hear me. No one believed me."

Her tears were flowing freely again. "I spent the whole day at the police station—and all it did was turn me into their prime suspect."

"But they let you leave?"

"Oh, sure. I told them where I was going, gave them the address, phone number, everything. They know they could have me picked up." She snapped her fingers. "Like that. And they advised me of my rights while I was being questioned. But I thought, why should I care since I'm telling the truth? Before I left Portland, Janice Doyle strongly suggested I get legal counsel. But why? I mean I'm innocent. Why do I need a lawyer?" She looked at him with teary eyes. *"Why?"*

"I don't know."

"Last night, after a long day of questioning, the police told me I was free to go. And I was a total mess," she admitted. "All I could think was that I wanted to come home. I wanted my parents. I'd called home the night before, but when no one answered I didn't want to leave a message. I was so upset, I knew my mom would fall apart, too. So I left a message on my dad's work phone. I totally forgot they were gone." She burst into more tears and, with no words to say, he just let her cry.

"I'm not usually such a crybaby," she finally told him. "But I feel so lost…so alone. A rumor started a while back—I'm certain from Brock—that I was angry at Kestra for stealing my boyfriend. I heard two coworkers whispering about it, but other than some irritation, I wrote it off as nothing. Of course, it was a natural conclusion that, because of my envy, I must've murdered Kestra in a jealous fit of rage." She shook her fists in the air. "That is such a lie! If I wanted to kill someone I'd kill Brock." Her fists fell to her lap. "But I wouldn't. I couldn't."

"Wow." Logan set down his pen. "That's a lot to take in. A lot for you to have gone through. And so recently, too."

She barely nodded.

"So, really, who do you think killed Kestra?"

She locked eyes with him again. "I think it was Brock.

Oh, not with his own hands since we all know that wasn't possible."

"Due to his alibi of being on the news?"

"Yes, but I still feel certain he was involved."

"I guess I don't understand why, Mallory. If he was going out with Kestra, and you said she seemed happy in that relationship, what motive would he have for killing her—or having someone else kill her? And so brutally, too?"

Her brow creased. "This was my biggest question, too. *Why?* I mean Kestra was still into him. As far as I knew, he hadn't gotten rough with her yet. She was still singing his praises. It makes no sense."

"So, why, then?"

Mallory's expression grew intense. "What I really think happened—and this is what I told the police just yesterday, but I know they don't believe me—but what I really think happened is that Brock meant for me to be killed."

Logan watched her closely, studying her intently. She seemed utterly sincere, and yet this accusation seemed even further out than the one that Brock had hired someone to murder his girlfriend.

"You see, Kestra was killed around 6:30 in my studio apartment. Normally, I get home from work around six—and that's after a nearly twelve-hour day—so I'm pretty worn out, and I usually take a nap as soon as I get home. Brock knows all about this. Then, if I'm planning to go out or anything, it's usually later. But if you want to find me between six and seven, I'm usually in my apartment. The news is usually on, and although I like to think I'm watching it, I'm usually snoozing."

"So where were you on this particular Wednesday?"

"At the Rose Garden." She let out a long sigh.

"The Rose Garden? Did anyone see you there?"

"No…and that's just what the police asked me. And Detective Snyder is like, *what a convenient alibi, she says she's off walking in the Rose Garden, all by herself, yeah, right.* But it's true, I was. It was a gorgeous summer day and I'd heard how pretty the roses were looking last week, and instead of going directly home, I treated myself to an evening stroll through The Rose Garden. Bad timing... I know."

Now she explained how the security cam by her apartment had something tossed over the lens to block it. And the knife that had been used to kill Kestra was from Mallory's kitchen, and according to police, it had a few of Mallory's prints on it. "But wouldn't everything in my house have my prints on it?"

"Seems like it."

"Even so, I think they're building their case around all that. Circumstantial evidence."

"But the police didn't keep you in custody."

She shook her head. "I almost wish they had."

"For safety?"

"Yeah."

"So you think Brock sent someone to your apartment to kill you." Logan suddenly remembered something. "Hey, those photos of you and Kestra in the newspaper, I couldn't help but notice you're both brunettes, similar hairstyles, similar look."

"Yeah."

"So maybe the murderer really did mistake Kestra for you?"

"That's my theory. I'm guessing Kestra came by to change clothes for something she was doing in town later that night. I think she'd let herself in...and then...well, you know the rest."

Logan put a hand on her shoulder. "I can't imagine how hard this has been for you, Mallory. To lose your best friend and then be accused of her murder. What a nightmare."

"A nightmare that won't end," she said sadly. "I really

wanted to talk to my dad about it. I should probably go ahead and call him now. Except I hate to ruin his vacation."

"Well, I have to inform him about the arson fire. I already left him a message, but I didn't go into details about—" His words were interrupted by a loud bang that made them both jump and Mallory grabbed him by the arm, cowering next to him.

"Was that a gunshot?" she whispered.

Already on high alert and concerned about the same thing, he scoped the perimeter of the park until he spotted an old yellow pickup turning a corner. "Oh, that's just Barry Jackson." He tried to sound unconcerned as he pointed across the park and stood. "His '55 Chevy backfires sometimes." But even as he said this, he wasn't so sure. It sounded more like a gunshot than a backfire.

He took her hand and guided her over to a clump of trees, watching over his shoulder as they went. Within the protective shadows of the trees, he gauged the situation. But seeing nothing out of the ordinary and sensing she was really on edge, Logan smiled uneasily. "You really need a break," he said gently. "You know what they say about stress."

"Huh?" She frowned.

"It's a killer." He pushed a strand of dark hair away from her eyes. He knew it was premature, but he suddenly felt like kissing her. Instead, he let his hand slowly trail down her cheek and around her chin. He was rewarded by a shy smile.

"You're right. The stress is really getting to me," she admitted. "But what can I do?"

"I'm not sure, but I do think we should move along." Even if it had only been a backfire, Logan felt worried. What if it had been a gun? Perhaps just a warning…for now, anyway.

He looked at his watch. "I've got to get over to the station for a while. I need to finish my reports and talk to Rod—he's my second in command. His shift starts today and goes until Monday. Then I'm back on again." He explained how the 24/7, four days on, three days off shift worked. "Why don't you come to the station with me?"

Mallory seemed uncertain.

"You could just hang out there while I do some office work. Probably take an hour or two."

"Will that woman—uh, Winnie—be there?"

Logan frowned. "Most likely."

"Maybe I'll take a pass."

"Okay." He made an apologetic smile and a mental note to give Winnie a quiet but firm reprimand.

"You know, what I'd really like to do is get a few things in town." Mallory ran her hands over her skirt, which looked more than a little rumpled. "This outfit is all I have to wear. I considered borrowing some of my mom's things." She wrinkled her nose.

"Except that your mom's a lot shorter and wider than you." As Logan attempted to keep the conversation light—for Mallory's sake—his eyes were skimming the perimeters of the park. Despite their peaceful surroundings, something felt off. And the hairs on the back of his neck felt prickly.

"So maybe I'll head over to Jorgenson's Sporting Goods," she said. "I could probably find a few things to get me through the weekend. I don't need much since I'm supposed to be back in Portland on Monday morning, for further interrogation I assume. Not that I want to think about that right now."

"I'm happy to drop you at the sporting-goods store."

"I can walk. It's just over—"

"No, I'll drive you." He gave the park another quick look before he led her to the truck.

"I could probably waste about an hour or more in there,"

she said. "If there's more time, I'll pop over to the drugstore and pick up a few other things I left behind."

"How about I meet you in front of the drugstore at three," Logan offered as he opened the passenger door for her. "If that works."

"Sounds perfect." She looked at him with grateful eyes. "I don't know how to thank you for everything. I honestly don't know what I'd have done without you today. You've been very kind and it's hard to believe that it's all in the line of duty."

Still wary and watching, he hurried around to the driver's side. "Well, some of it's in the line of duty," he admitted as he slid behind the wheel. "And the part that's not is in the line of pleasure."

She rewarded him with a smile.

"I know this feels like a never-ending nightmare to you, but I still believe that good can come out of evil, Mallory. When you love God and put your trust in him."

"Really? You honestly believe that?" Her voice sounded hopeful. "I want to believe that, too, Logan. But it's been so hard lately. Really, really hard."

"Well, maybe I can just believe it for you. For now, anyway." He longed to protect her as he started the engine. "Things are going to get better." But even as he said this, he felt unsure. Before they got better, it was possible that they could get a whole lot worse.

It was hard enough dropping her off in front of the sporting-goods store—even though the street was busy with shoppers he knew by first name—the idea of allowing Mallory to return to her parents' home where some deranged criminal was lurking in the woods, waiting for his chance to take her out…well, it was more than a little disturbing. As Logan drove to the fire station he knew he needed to come up with a better solution—before it was too late!

SEVEN

It didn't take long for Mallory to gather up some suitable small-town clothes. A pair of jeans, khaki walking shorts, a couple of T-shirts, a flannel shirt and a sweatshirt. Not exactly city clothes—not for someone who wanted to be taken seriously as a career girl, that is. Although that might not matter so much anymore. For, as far as she knew, her career was over. At least she'd have something to wear during the time she was hiding out here in Clover. She found a few other things, too, including a pair of hiking shoes and some sturdy sandals.

"Do you mind if I put some of these on?" she asked the salesgirl helping her. "More comfy than this outfit, you know?"

"No problem, let me cut off the tags for you."

Dressed in a light blue T-shirt, khaki shorts and sandals, Mallory felt almost like she belonged in Clover again as she headed across the street to the drugstore. She hadn't been in this store for years, but remembered how she and her best friend, Leah, used to love studying the cosmetics counter as teens. Funny how her beauty routine had gotten much simpler once she was able to afford all that stuff. She picked out the few items she was missing, then made her way to the checkout stand.

"Mallory Myers!" the middle-aged woman behind the cash register exclaimed. "What are you doing here?"

"Shopping." Mallory smiled at Wanda Snow as she set her basket on the counter.

"I haven't seen you in ages."

"I know. How are you doing?" Mallory asked as a woman with a toddler in a stroller got in line behind her.

"I'm just fine, honey. It's good to see you. But I'm surprised you're in town. I thought your mom told me they were going on vacation last week—"

"That's right. I'm guessing they're in Iowa by now." Mallory unloaded the items from her basket, suppressing the urge to frown. "To my dad's family reunion." How she wished they hadn't gone.

"Isn't that nice."

The woman behind Mallory kept leaning over her stroller, acting as though she was impatient to be checked out or trying to get something from the rack next to the register. Finally Mallory turned to face the woman. "Did you need something?" she asked with polite curiosity.

"You *are* Mallory Myers!" the woman blurted out.

"That's right."

The woman's narrow brows arched and she stepped back ever so slightly—almost as if she was intimidated or afraid. "I—uh—I just read about you in the paper."

"You're in the newspaper?" Wanda set a bottle of hair conditioner in the bag.

"Well, I wouldn't—"

"It's right here!" The pushy woman reached past Mallory to get a newspaper from a stack next to the checkout stand. She triumphantly held it up for Mrs. Snow to see. "Today's *Mid-State News*—front page, too!"

Wanda adjusted her reading glasses and peered at the paper. "Oh, my!" She looked at Mallory with an alarmed expression.

"That headline is a big fat lie." Mallory zipped her debit card through the reader. "Just someone's idea of a sensational story. A good way to sell newspapers." She snatched up a paper and slapped it on the counter. "See it works, too, I'll buy this. But trust me, it's not true."

"Well, of course, it's not true." Wanda dropped moisturizer in the bag. "It couldn't possibly be true. Anyone who knows you would know it's not true." She smiled uneasily as she handed Mallory her receipt.

"Thank you," Mallory said. "Have a good day." As she hurried outside, she wondered if this was such a good idea…hanging around in town like this until Logan returned for her. Part of her felt safe here. Who would dare to hurt her with so many people around to witness it? The other part of her felt conspicuous…and embarrassed. There was more than one way to be hurt.

She found an empty bench next to the drugstore and, sitting down on the shady end, she removed the newspaper. The *Mid-State News* was not known for its accuracy in reporting. But insinuating she was a murderer almost seemed grounds for libel. Opening it up, she attempted to conceal herself behind the paper screen as she skimmed the sensational front-page story. Just as she expected, the editors had been somewhat careful. Rather than outright accusations within the article, they used words like "alleged" and "possible suspect." They obviously wanted to avoid a defamation-of-character suit. Even so, the headline was nasty and the article made her look bad. Very bad.

"Excuse me," a deep voice said.

She peeked over the top of the paper to see a muscular pale-haired man standing in front of her. She knew by his tan-and-brown uniform he was with the sheriff's department, just like her dad. "Yes?" She attempted a weak smile. She'd always felt comfortable around law enforcement before, but so many things had changed since Wednesday.

And for some reason—maybe it was his wide-legged stance or that superior expression—but this guy made her uneasy.

"Miss Myers?"

"Yes." She lowered the paper, returning what felt like an intense look, although she couldn't be certain since his eyes were concealed behind his dark aviator glasses.

"Mind if I join you?"

She shrugged uneasily. "No, of course, not." She bit her tongue to keep from saying "It's a free country." This didn't seem the sort of man to get sassy with. Not to mention, she should've learned a few lessons from the Portland police.

He eased himself down on the bench then turned to her with what seemed a disingenuous smile. "I know all about you, Miss Myers."

She just nodded, realizing what this was about. "I'm sure you *think* you do."

His faux smile vanished. "What do you mean by *that*?"

She held up the paper. "I guess it all depends on where you get your information."

"I'm with the sheriff's department," he said with what sounded like plain old arrogance. "For your information, we're not limited to news media sources. Everyone knows that the media is unreliable."

She pursed her lips. Was he aware that she was a news writer?

"Trust me, Miss Myers. I do my research. And I do know all about you."

"Just because you've researched doesn't mean you got the *full* story. And your claim that you know *all about me* convinces me that you know diddly-squat."

When he didn't respond, Mallory began to feel nervous. What had she been thinking? Sparring with a lawman? She knew better! "I'm sorry," she blurted out. "I seem to have gotten off on the wrong foot here. The truth is, I was just feeling seriously aggravated by this newspaper article." She narrowed her eyes at him as she tossed the paper to the bench.

He nodded to the rumpled paper. "It's quite a story."

Now she pointed to his name tag. "Okay, you seem to know who I am, Deputy Fallows, but I don't believe we've officially met." She stuck out her hand. "I suspect you know my dad, Deputy Myers. Doesn't that make us sort of like family?" She attempted an authentic smile, but couldn't quite manage it.

He gave her a limp handshake that didn't match his macho-man physique and sent a creepy feeling down her spine.

"So, what can I do for you, Deputy Fallows?" she asked nervously. Hopefully he didn't have a warrant for her arrest. She knew that could happen. The detectives had warned her it could.

"I just figured I should make my presence known to you. I've already been in contact with Portland, and I know that they're trying to keep you on a short leash. Frankly I'm surprised they allowed you to leave town at all. But I assured Detective Snyder I'd be keeping a close eye on you."

"Oh, good." The sarcasm leaped back into her voice. "I'm such a flight risk."

His brow creased as if he was taking her seriously. "I do have a question for you, Miss Myers. It's regarding the arson incident near your parents' home last night."

"What do you want to know?" she asked.

"It seems a strange coincidence that you show up at your parents' home late in the night. And then a fire erupts shortly after you get there. And I can't help but wonder why you're coming here when you know your parents are away on a road trip."

"I forgot about that."

"Yeah, maybe so. Especially considering how busy you've been lately. Seems like everywhere you go, excitement follows. Murder, arson... What's next, Miss Myers?"

"For your information, that fire that was probably started by the same person who committed the murder." She glared at him.

He rubbed a line of sweat from his upper lip and shrugged. "If the shoe fits."

"What's that supposed to mean?"

"I mean that I'll be keeping my eye on you, Miss Myers." He slowly stood. "Now if you'll excuse—"

"Wait a minute." Mallory jumped to her feet, standing in front of this impudent deputy. "Are you seriously suggesting that *I* set that fire last night?"

"No offense, little lady, but it seems like a pretty good smoke screen to me."

"A *smoke screen*?"

He chuckled. "Sure. Even now, you're suggesting it's the work of that diabolical murderer, claiming that he chased you all the way to Clover. A clever means to convince the Portland detectives that you're the one in danger, that you didn't really murder your friend."

"That is absurd."

"Not really." He seemed to smirk. "I've been going over all the details of your case. It actually makes a lot of sense."

"Except that you're dead wrong." She knew it was probably foolish get on this guy's bad side, but she felt like she was already sliding down the slippery slope. Even so, she attempted to soften her expression and tone down her voice. "I'm telling you the truth, Deputy Fallows, I had nothing to do with my friend's death or last night's fire. I'm innocent."

"Just because your daddy is a deputy doesn't mean you'll find sanctuary or extra sympathy here in Clover. If you were smart you'd go back to Portland."

Mallory wanted to throw something at this surly creep. He reminded her of Brock. As if these two were cut from the same cloth. Was it possible they knew each other? Had

Brock been in touch with Deputy Fallows? "Before you leave," she said quickly, "I have a question for you."

"What's that?" he asked impatiently.

"Do you happen to be on friendly terms with Brock Dennison?"

One side of his mouth twitched ever so slightly, but he didn't answer. "Speaking of friends, I hear you're getting pretty cozy with our fire chief."

"Are you going to tell me who I can or cannot be friends with now?"

He pointed to where a bright red Jeep Wrangler was pulling up right in front of the drugstore. "Hail, hail the chief." He laughed, waving as Logan climbed out of the Jeep. He'd changed from his uniform into a casual pair of faded jeans and a gray T-shirt, and he was smiling as he casually strolled toward them.

"What's up?" Logan looked from Mallory to the deputy with curious interest.

"I was just about to call you, Logan. But while I've got you both here, I might as well inform you of the news."

"What news?" Logan asked in a firm tone.

"That due to your friendly relationship with the little lady here, I will be taking over the arson investigation as of now."

"What are you talking—"

"Look, Logan, you've been spotted all over town with this girl. And due to her involvement in the Portland murder case combined with suspicions that she might be involved in last night's arson, it would be inappropriate for you to continue the investigation. Don'tcha think? Besides that, according to Winnie, you're not even on duty this weekend, anyway. So what's the big deal?"

"That's who you've been talking to." Logan's response was surprisingly calm. "Winnie Halston has shared her CSI theories with you. Now it all makes sense."

"What makes sense is for you to step away from last night's arson investigation. I'll be handling it from here on out. And I'll expect you to turn your findings over to me ASAP. Understand?"

"No problem." Logan's tone sounded agreeable, but Mallory thought she could see sparks burning in the backs of his deep green eyes. "One less investigation for me to bother with. You're welcome to it. Copies of my reports are on file in the computer at the station. Have at it." He reached for Mallory's elbow. "Ready to go?"

"Uh, yeah." She grabbed up her shopping bags and, grateful for Logan's calm presence, allowed him to guide her away from Deputy Fallows. Her head was still spinning from that crazy conversation. Had she really understood him correctly? It was bad enough when that ditzy firefighter woman made that embarrassing scene in the diner. But knowing Mallory now had the sheriff's department treating her like a suspect was truly alarming. It was bad enough in Portland, but here in her hometown? She wondered what her dad would think.

"Did you connect with my dad yet?" she asked as Logan slid into the driver's seat.

"No, but I left another message. I didn't go into all the details, but I told him it was urgent and that it involved you and your safety. And I asked him to call back as soon as possible. I figured that would get his attention."

"I hope so." Mallory sighed. "I think it's time to give Al Brandt a call."

"I'm inclined to agree with you. Even people who are innocent sometimes need a good attorney." Logan made a quick turn down Spruce Street. "Let's stop by and see if he's around."

To Mallory's great disappointment, Al was not there. According to the sign on the front door of the small law office, he'd be gone for several days on a fly-fishing trip and wouldn't be back until Tuesday. They were just leaving when Mallory's phone chimed. Wishing it was her dad, she pulled it out, only to discover it was a new text message. Another threat. "Oh, no," she said quietly.

"What's wrong?" Logan asked as he came to a stop sign.

Mallory looked all around, trying to see if anyone suspicious was lurking nearby. "This text, Logan. Listen to this—'Think you're safe in that little red Jeep? Think again. I've got my eye on you. And it's open season.'"

Like her, Logan looked all around. "Have you seen anyone in the past couple of hours? Anyone that made you suspicious?"

"You mean besides Deputy Fallows?" She felt a creepy chill running through her again. "The truth is, I don't feel like I can really trust anyone anymore."

"What about those text messages?" he asked. "Should you be sending them to the police?"

"I've been sending them to Portland," she explained as she stared at her phone. "Not that they take me seriously. Do you know what one of the detectives had the nerve to tell me?"

"No, what?"

"Apparently there's a new app or a device or something that you can use to send yourself texts and it makes it appear as if it's from someone else."

"Great," he said with sarcasm.

"I used to trust people," she said sadly. "I used to think that most cops were good people. That most journalists were honest. Now I don't know what to think—or who to trust. "

"You can trust me." Logan's brow creased as he peered into his rearview mirror. He was obviously worried about something. Perhaps the killer was stalking them right now. And why not? Out here in the open like this—they made easy targets. Suddenly Mallory got it—her friendship with

Logan was putting him at serious risk. She wasn't the only one in danger now. Somehow, as badly as she needed him and wanted him around, she needed to tell him to stay away from her. For his own sake.

EIGHT

As Logan drove cautiously through town, Mallory felt her heart racing. Imagining a sniper rifle pointed directly at the little red Jeep, she knew she had no right to endanger Logan like this. "I think you should take me home," she said suddenly. "And then stay away from me."

"I'm not comfortable with that." He looked around as he came to an intersection. "I've been giving this some serious consideration, trying to figure out where the safest place for you might be. I'd take you to my place, Mallory, but it's right in the center of town—not to mention my house isn't much of a fortress with an open floor plan and a ton of windows. TJ calls it the fishbowl. Besides that, everyone knows where I live and judging by that last text, it's no secret that you're with me. Do you have any ideas? I know you don't want to go back to Portland yet, but do you know anyone with a secure house around here? A place you can spend the night?"

"I've got some friends—rather, parents of friends—who live around here. But after that last text, I doubt that I'm safe anywhere. And if I'm not safe, it makes me seriously concerned for anyone I might be with." She glanced nervously at him. "Including you."

"Don't worry about me."

"I think it's best if I stay at my parents'."

"Really?"

She nodded firmly. "Yeah, I do. Especially if I can get hold of Dad and get the combination to his gun safe."

"Guns?" Logan sounded surprised.

"You know my dad's a lawman. He's also a hunter. Of course he's got guns." She checked her phone again, to see if her dad had called back yet. All she could think was that they were out of cell phone range because no way would they ignore her like this. Especially after the message Logan had left.

"Yes, I figured your dad has guns. But do *you* know how to handle a firearm?"

"Sure. My dad taught Austin and me to shoot when we were kids. We've been through all kinds of gun safety training, and I even have a concealed weapons permit, not that I use it. But I do happen to be a pretty good shot."

"Really...?" Logan sounded impressed. "As a matter of fact, so am I."

"Maybe we should go have ourselves a little shoot-out." She tried to insert some lightness into her voice by attempting a Western drawl. "My pa used to call me Annie Oakley. Think you can outshoot me, pardner?"

"Well, I reckon I'd like to give it a try." He imitated her accent as he turned into a parking lot, but she could tell he was looking all around as he slowly drove toward the town's only grocery store. He was obviously feeling just as cautious as she was.

"What are we doing here?" She used the side mirror to see if any vehicles had followed them in, but she only saw a blue minivan and a white convertible.

"For starters, it feels like a safe place to stop." He glanced around. "Easy to see people coming and going—and the sheriff's department is right across the street."

Mallory nodded. "Good point."

"I figure if someone's following us, they won't feel that comfortable around here."

"Makes sense." She looked over to the sheriff's department, remembering how she used to enjoy visiting there as a girl. But with deputies like Trent on the force, she wasn't so sure.

"Besides that, I figure if we're gonna hole up at your parents' place for a spell, with our firearms and whatnot, maybe we should get ourselves some provisions first." He winked at her. "That is, unless you want to hunt some squirrel or rabbit or possum for supper."

"No, thanks," she said as they got out of the car. "I can shoot just fine, but I've never been into hunting." As they went into the store, she tried to replay his words. Had he really insinuated that he planned to stay at her parents' home with her? Or had she heard him wrong? But as they gathered groceries, it was clear that he was picking out food that he intended to eat, so it seemed safe to assume that he meant to stick around.

As they made their way to the checkout stand, she looked around the store, curious as to whether anyone suspicious was following them, but nothing really caught her eye. As they went outside with the loaded cart, she noticed a dark vehicle parked off by itself, not far from the parking lot entrance and just out of sight of the sheriff's department. She elbowed Logan. "See that SUV?"

"Uh-huh." He nodded at her without looking at it.

"Do you think—" Her jangling phone interrupted her and as Logan began unloading the groceries, she answered it. To her huge relief it was her dad. "Oh, Daddy!" she cried. "I'm so glad to hear your voice."

"What's wrong?" he demanded. "That message Logan left had me so worried I didn't know what to think. And I didn't even tell your mom something was wrong. She's having such a good time visiting with your aunt Susan. I didn't want to send her into a conniption fit. What's going on there?"

As Logan continued loading the bags, Mallory got inside and, keeping one eye on the dark SUV through the side mirror, she poured out the whole story as best she could, starting with the murder and her suspicions of Brock. She was explaining about the arson as Logan got into the driver's seat. "I really thought I'd be safe here, Dad. In my hometown. I thought Clover would be different than Portland."

"It'd be different if I was there. I think your mom and I should come home right now and—"

"I hate to ruin your vacation...your time with your family."

"But I can't enjoy it if I'm worried about you. This is a very serious situation. And I never wanted to say it, but I was always suspicious of Brock Dennison. Even though we never met face-to-face, he's always seemed a little phony to me. And looks like I was right. Smooth charm on the outside, but a slimy snake underneath."

"That sounds about right."

"Do you really think he's a murderer?"

She explained about his rock-solid alibi. "And that's why I thought I was safe from him, Dad. I figured I could watch him on the news and know that he wasn't out there hiding in the woods, ready to pounce."

"But if your theory is right, it sounds like Brock got someone else to do his dirty work." Her dad blew out a long sigh. "That just makes me sick, Mallory. I can hardly believe it. But my point is this, if whoever killed Kestra botched his assignment, he might be even more determined to get to you. I really don't like this, Mallory. We're coming home."

"I can't tell you what to do, Dad. But in the meantime, I'd like the combination to your gun safe. Logan and I feel

it's safest to hole up at the house, but we'd feel better if
we're armed. You know?"

"I agree. But I wish I was there right now." He gave her
the combo, and she wrote it on her palm. "Just promise
me you'll be super careful—remember everything you've
learned about gun safety."

"I promise. And Logan's familiar with firearms, too."
She noticed the dark SUV moving now, it looked as if it
was about to leave. She nudged Logan, and he just nodded
with a nonchalant expression, munching on a chip.

"It's reassuring to know Logan is there with you. He's a
good man. But I still plan to get home as soon as possible,
Mallory. Unfortunately that'll take a couple days, even if
we drive nonstop."

"Don't do that, Dad."

"I'm coming home, Mallory. Don't try to talk me out of
it. Seems my only option is to get the soonest flight possible. As soon as I hang up, I'll check on a red-eye. Maybe
I can be there by morning. I'll leave your mom here, then
fly back to rejoin her when I know you're safe."

Mallory looked at Logan. "Do what you need to, Dad.
And please don't worry Mom too much, okay?" Mallory
knew how sick her mother could get over worrying.

"I'll call you from the airport. And as soon as I hang up
here, I'll give my deputy buddies a call. Ask them to be on
high alert for you."

Of course, that reminded her of the deputy she'd met
today, and she told her dad about the weird encounter. "It
was pretty disturbing. I mean, I thought I'd be safe in Clover, and then this deputy acts like he's going to arrest me."

"Between you and me, I don't trust Trent Fallows. Every
once in a while there's a bad cop—kinda like a bad apple—
and he starts to spoil everything. That's what Trent Fallows
is. Anyway, I'll text you my buddies' phone numbers and
you put them in your phone. You call them directly if you

need help. Not the 911 dispatcher—because if you do, it's likely that you'll just get Fallows."

"Don't call 911." She repeated his directions loudly as Logan drove out into the street. "Got it."

"Not that you can't trust the dispatchers, but if Trent's on duty…well, he's been under investigation for a while now. But you keep that to yourself, you hear?"

"You can trust me, Daddy."

"I do trust you. But I have one big question for you. Something you haven't fully answered—at least, not to me. But it's something you need to sort out if you're going to resolve this mess."

"What's that?"

"If you're right about Brock, if that snake really is behind Kestra's murder, and if it was a case of mistaken identity and Brock really wanted you dead—you need to ask yourself *why*. Why does he want you dead? I know he didn't want to let you go, Mallory, I get that. But is that really his motive? No offense, honey, but that just doesn't sit right with me. It seems too extreme. Brock is full of himself. He loves his big newscaster image. And I suspect he's a narcissist. For him to risk everything by hiring a hit man doesn't make sense. Not just for being jilted."

"I'm sure you're right." She looked both ways at the next intersection, trying to see if she could spot that SUV. "Especially about the narcissist assessment."

"A narcissist doesn't want to look bad."

"I did make him look bad…by dumping him."

"But didn't you say he pretended to be the dumper?"

"That's true." She sneaked a chip from Logan's bag.

"So ask yourself…was there anything else you did in your relationship that threatened Brock in such a huge way that he'd want you snuffed out? Something in the workplace maybe? An incident where you embarrassed him?

Made him look bad in front of the boss? Tweaked his big narcissist ego some way?"

Mallory thought hard as she munched. "Brock got really aggravated at me when I was working on a dating and domestic violence story. I told him what I was doing and he got all indignant, like, why did we need to run a story like that? So I reminded him of an accusation against a local college football player and how this was a follow-up story." She shook her head to remember how Brock had belittled her.

"Bingo."

"You really think so?"

"It could be the missing puzzle piece. You definitely need to look into it. And I need to get off the phone and book a flight. You be safe now, Mallory. I love you, honey."

"I love you, too, Dad."

"Be sure to thank Logan for me. I know you're in good hands with him—until I get there."

After she hung up, she followed her dad's directions by thanking Logan.

"Sorry to eavesdrop," Logan said in a serious tone, "but I'd like to hear more about that dating and domestic violence story and how it relates to Brock."

"Oh…right. So as I researched for that piece, I started to wonder if Brock might possibly have a history as an abuser. Like maybe he'd grown up in a home with domestic violence. I gently asked him about this and even suggested he might need some counseling. And, man, did he blow up on me. You'd have thought I'd suggested he was serial killer."

"Sounds like he has something to hide. Did you do any research on him specifically? Check out *his* past?"

"No…" She had meant to do that, but everything in their relationship had been so volatile and scary at the time, she'd put most of her energy into safely exiting that relationship.

"Maybe you need to do more research. Sniff out whatever he's trying to hide. If Brock's image is that important to him, it makes sense that he wouldn't want you to expose any dirty secrets, and if he's as crazy as you're suggesting, that could be his motive to shut you up."

"Yeah," she said quietly. "My dad hinted at the same thing." She knew that putting these pieces together should've been encouraging—on some level. But it mostly just reinforced her fear. She glanced at Logan, wishing she hadn't involved him in her mess. "I know Dad's really grateful for your help, Logan. And so am I. But if he gets a red-eye flight, he should be here by morning. And you can be off the hook and out of harm's—"

"Look what's up ahead," Logan said in a somber tone. They were on the back road now, still about ten minutes from her parents' house.

"That same SUV," she said with apprehension.

"Get down in the seat," he said quickly. "Keep your head below the door line."

"But I—"

"Now!" He reached over and pushed her head down. "Sorry. But my reason is twofold. One, they might assume you're not still with me and, two, they might be armed."

"What about *you*?" she demanded as she remained hunched over, her head in her lap.

"Don't worry. Just hang on. I'm going to step on it, see if I can blast past and just lose them." He hit the gas and the Jeep took off. "Or maybe we're just paranoid and they're not really waiting for us."

"What's happening?" she asked after about a minute of hunkering down. She knew they were still at least six or seven miles from the turnoff to her parents' house and this was a fairly isolated road.

"The SUV pulled out behind us," he told her. "They're coming at us fast."

"Did you get the license?"

"Couldn't see it. Stay down." He went even faster now.

Everything in her wanted to poke her head up and peek out, but she respected him too much to disobey his orders—besides that, she was scared. "What's going on?" she demanded as she felt the Jeep slowing down. "What's wrong?"

"The SUV caught up. No chance I can outrun it. They're tailing like they want to turn us into their hood ornament. So close that I can't see the license plate, but it's got one of those plastic covers that makes it hard to read. It's a late-model black Durango with tinted glass, so I can't see inside. Stay down and brace yourself, I think he's getting ready to ram into us."

"Ram into?" Just then she felt a hard jolt from behind. "They hit your Jeep?" she cried. "Why are they doing that?"

"Trying to get us to stop. This does not look good."

She felt another jolt from behind, but instead of screaming out as she felt like doing, she reached for her phone. If this was the killer who murdered Kestra—the arsonist who set last night's fire—there was no telling what he'd do next. So, despite her dad's warning, she dialed 911. What else could she do until she got the numbers of Dad's buddies? She had barely explained the situation to the female dispatcher when the Jeep was rammed again, this time knocking the vehicle completely off the road, and the phone tumbled from her hand.

Mallory felt the Jeep tilting to one side as if it was about to roll. She screamed.

NINE

"Hang on, Mallory," Logan yelled, "we're about to go four-wheeling." Holding tightly onto the wheel, he steadied the Jeep out, getting all four wheels back onto the rough terrain. Relieved not to have rolled, he noticed a good-sized opening in the woods and took it, hoping it would run into an old logging road. There were a number of them throughout the National Forest. He and his friends had often taken their four-wheel-drive vehicles out on days like this just for the fun of it. He felt a sense of satisfaction when then citified SUV couldn't follow.

"Did we lose them?" Mallory asked from where she was still bent over, grasping the sides of the seat with both hands.

"They stopped at the turn. I wish they would follow." He kept his focus on the terrain in front of him as the Jeep bounced along, searching for an old dirt road. "Their SUV was one of those city rigs, low to the ground. This rough ride would tear it apart."

"Can I sit up now?"

He glanced in the rearview mirror and saw nothing but trees behind them. "Sure," he said as they bumped along. "We lost them…for now."

"I was calling 911 after they hit us, but I lost my phone." She bent down, feeling around on the floor.

"I thought your dad said no 911 calls."

"I know, but I was so scared—and I didn't have those other phone numbers yet." She held up her phone victoriously. "The call's still live." And suddenly she was talking to the dispatcher. "We managed to lose the vehicle," she said, describing how they'd been hit from behind and knocked off the road. And then she gave a fairly good description of the SUV.

"How about if you talk to Logan?" she was saying. "He can fill you in better." She held the phone out to him and he slowed to a stop as he took it.

"This Logan McDaniel," he said in a crisp business-like voice.

"Hello, Chief. This is Barbara Hiller. What exactly is going on out there in the woods? Where are you now? And where are you headed?"

He gave the general location. "I'm not sure what the SUV had in mind," he admitted, "but we felt our lives were in real danger. The hits were intentional, and I'm sure they wanted me to stop. As far as where we're headed…" He looked around. "I'm not sure. We might just lie low until the sheriff's department gets that SUV. Sorry I couldn't get a license number, but there can't be too many rigs like that in these parts. And Mallory forgot to mention it was a low-rider. Tinted windows and a plastic-covered license plate. Should be easy to identify it."

"I'll pass that along right now, sir."

"We'll find a safe spot to just chill for a while," he told her. "You call us back when you find out something or the thugs are picked up. Either this number or my cell phone."

"I'll let you know as soon as I hear anything. And you be sure to call back if you have any more trouble."

"Thanks, Barbara." He disconnected the call and handed the phone back.

He drove a wide circle that took them a mile or so from

her parents' house, but without using the main road. Hopefully, the black SUV would be picked up before long.

"Where are we?" she asked when he finally came to a stop.

"Not far from home." He pointed south. "Your parents' place is less than a mile from here."

"I thought it looked familiar."

He glanced at his phone. "It's been almost thirty minutes since our nasty encounter. I'm surprised the dispatcher hasn't called back."

Mallory seemed to relax now, leaning into the car seat. "It's so peaceful here… I really don't mind just hanging out for a while. The view is beautiful."

He looked out at the afternoon sunlight filtering like gold through the pine trees. Very pretty. Now he shifted in his seat and, leaning back into the door, he studied Mallory's profile, the curve of her cheek, the way the loose dark hair framed her face. "Yeah…you're right," he said quietly. *"Beautiful."*

She turned to look at him and, realizing he was watching her, gave a self-conscious smile. "Huh?"

"You are."

"What?"

"Beautiful."

She tipped her head to one side. "Really? Well, thank you."

Now he decided to take a risk. Reaching out, he touched her face again, gently pulling her toward him. And when their lips met, she did not resist. It was just as sweet as he'd imagined. But suddenly his phone was jangling in his pocket.

"Oh," she said, pulling back. "You better answer that."

He pulled the phone out and said a reluctant hello.

"Hey, Chief, this Barbara again. Good news. They stopped the SUV. It was just like you described. They've taken the driver in for questioning, and I can't give you all the details, but it sounds like they found enough contraband to hold him."

"Fantastic!" he exclaimed. "The best news I've heard all day."

"So the coast is clear," Barbara assured him.

He thanked her and hung up, quickly sharing the good news with Mallory. "Looks like we can take you home now."

"Great." She smiled, but he sensed that, like him, she would've been happy to have remained there a while. Still, it felt as though the moment had passed. And it would probably be wise to get her safely to her parents' house. Just because one man had been taken into custody didn't guarantee her troubles were over.

"Do you think this will be the end of it?" she asked as they bumped along through the woods. "I mean the end of the threats… I realize I still need to clear my name…and I need to figure out if I'm right about Brock."

"I feel hopeful," he told her. "If the guy driving the SUV was the guy who murdered your friend, I would think that you'd be safe." But even as he said this, he wasn't so sure.

She pulled out her phone again. "I think I'll text my dad about this."

"Good idea."

"And I'll ask for his computer password," she said as she texted. "So I can do some more research—collect more information for the police before I talk to them again on Monday."

"Makes sense."

"And you probably don't need to stick around and be my protector now," she said in a light tone.

"Well, how about if I stick around and just be your friend," he suggested as her parents' house came into sight through the trees.

"Great. I was hoping that you would at least want to stay for dinner. Especially since you picked out most of the groceries. Those steaks looked pretty good."

"Wild horses couldn't pull me away," he said as he parked next to her car in the driveway.

"The place looks just like we left it," she said as they got out.

"Yep." He looked all around, trying to quell the feeling of anxiety that was still with him. As much as he wanted to believe they were out of harm's way, he just wasn't sure.

Together they carried the groceries into the house and then he helped her to unload the bags. This ordinary task brought a sense of normality with it, as if Mallory was just an ordinary girl…not someone in danger, someone suspected of murder.

"I wonder if I should tell Dad not to come," Mallory said as she put the lettuce in the vegetable cooler. "If the guy in the SUV is the killer, and he's locked up, there's no reason for my dad to leave his family reunion."

"Except that he's your dad, he's worried about you and he probably wants to be here to help you. And even if they picked up the killer, what about your theory about Brock Dennison? He's still out there, still able to create havoc… or worse."

She held up her hands. "But what if I'm wrong about him? I'm actually starting to question myself. What if I've made a mountain out of a molehill?" She turned away to gaze out the kitchen window. "Maybe I should tell Dad to wait before booking a flight."

"Based on what you've told me…and after reading the newspaper article, I think you have good reason to be extremely cautious when it comes to Brock Dennison. And I plan to keep my word to your dad. I'm not leaving you alone, Mallory." He pulled an apple out of the bag and bit into it. As he chewed, he heard a phone jingling. "Sounds like that's yours," he said. "Maybe your dad got a flight."

She went for her purse, eagerly extracting her phone and then staring down at it with a troubled expression. "Oh, no!"

"What is it?" He hurried over to see a text. Like the others it was from "unknown."

Think you're safe now? Think again. I've got my eye on you. And your boyfriend too.

"How is that possible?" Mallory demanded. "The guy is in custody, right?"

"That's right…according to the dispatcher."

"Can you trust her?"

"Sure." Logan nodded. "She's a friend of my mom's."

"Then who sent this?" She held up her phone.

"Is it from Brock?"

"But how can he be watching me if he's in Portland?"

"Are you certain he's in Portland?"

She frowned. "Well, he should be on the news tonight. That's live."

"So maybe this isn't from him." Logan studied the words. "Should I assume that I'm the boyfriend they're referring to?"

She made a nervous smile. "I wouldn't mind."

He pulled her close, looking down into her eyes. "I wouldn't mind, either."

"Except that you're in danger when you're with me," she said quietly.

"It's worth it." He kissed her again. She returned his kiss, but suddenly she pulled away.

"If someone is really watching us…" She glanced nervously out a window. "Shouldn't we be more careful?"

"Careful?"

"I mean prepared." She nodded her head toward the

other end of the house. "Time for me to show you my dad's arsenal."

Mallory reached for a bear-shaped cookie jar that was never used for cookies and retrieved the brass key taped inside the lid. "I'll show you the bear cave."

"Bear cave." He chuckled. "I like the sound of that."

"So does my dad. It's his special place." She led him down the hallway. "Come to think of it, it's probably the safest room in the house." She unlocked the door and turned on the overhead light, pointing up to the high, narrow windows covered with wooden blinds. They didn't even open. "Welcome to Dad's bear cave."

Logan clicked the dead bolt locked. "Very secure."

"The dead bolt is because of this." She patted Dad's big, dark green gun safe. "And he stores his ammo in here, too." To prove this she opened a wall cabinet that was well stocked with various boxes of shells and bullets and reloading equipment. "Dad always keeps this room locked tight when he's not home."

"He's a very responsible guy."

Mallory studied the combination on her hand then proceeded to turn the dial. After a couple of tries, the gun safe opened.

"Wow." Logan looked at the firearms with appreciation. "Impressive collection."

She reached in to get the two guns that belonged to her. Both were gifts from her dad and what she used when they went target shooting. Dad had given her the .22 rifle for her fourteenth birthday because it wasn't too big for her to handle. And the walnut-handled pistol and leather holster came later on. Although it had been a few years since she'd shot, these guns felt familiar in her hands. She laid them on the coffee table and frowned. "I wonder if we really need these now."

"I hope not."

While Logan perused the gun safe, she went to the ammo cabinet, retrieving several boxes of the appropriate bullets and setting them by her guns.

"These should work for me." Logan laid her dad's black AR-15 rifle and a sturdy-looking Ruger handgun next to hers.

"Help yourself." She waved her hand across the ammo cabinet as if she was the hostess of a game show.

Logan chuckled as he looked through the assorted boxes until he located the right sized bullets. "These will do." He set them on the table then stood back to look. "Nice little arsenal we've assembled."

"My dad always says that if you have to shoot, you should shoot to kill." She shuddered to think of this. "But I'm not sure I really have that in me."

"Maybe it's best not to think about it." He took one last bite of his apple then tossed the core into the trash can next to the desk. "Let's just be prepared and hope that it's unnecessary." He yawned.

"Yeah." Mallory studied him as he opened a box of ammo. She wasn't sure when he'd last shaved, but he had those rugged good looks that made a stubble beard attractive. Still, it was a reminder that he'd put in a long night—probably a long week, too. "You must be exhausted," she said. "How about getting a little afternoon nap while I do some research on Dad's computer?"

"That's probably a good idea. I'd like to be wide awake this evening. I have a feeling that if anyone is going to attempt anything, it'll be after dark." He frowned. "But I really don't want to leave you alone—even while I'm sleeping."

"This is the safest room in the house," she reminded him as she unlocked the door. "And I'll even lock the dead bolt if that makes you feel better."

"It does."

"And the guest room is right next to it." She pointed to the door. "Why not just make yourself comfortable there? If by any chance I need you, I can call your phone or bang on the wall or scream or whatever."

"You promise?" He put his face close to hers.

"I promise." She smiled.

"Because I don't want anything to happen to you."

"Same back at you. But I think we'll both be better off if you have a nap." She pointed to a well-worn suede couch in the bear cave. "And if I get sleepy, I'll just use that. It's where the Papa Bear usually hibernates."

He nodded, still standing in the doorway. "Okay. Just don't forget to dead bolt the door."

"I won't." She went over to the desk, sitting down in her dad's chair and turning on the computer.

"I overheard your dad's advice," Logan said sleepily. "For you to research Brock's past…that's a good idea."

"Yeah, I can't believe I didn't think of it myself." She plugged in the password her dad had texted back to her and went online.

"I'll admit I was curious about the same thing. Why would Brock go to such an extreme? Murder someone just for being dumped? I mean, sure, I'd be upset to be dumped by a girl like you…but murder? Not so much."

She turned to look at him standing in the doorway… looking relaxed and almost at home. He let out a sleepy yawn and pointed to the dead bolt again. "Don't forget."

"Have a good nap," she told him as she got up, closed the door and secured the lock. She leaned against the door and sighed. Logan was such a great guy. Why hadn't their paths crossed before this? She leaned against the door for a full minute, just replaying the events of the day, the kisses they'd exchanged this afternoon. It was all so unexpected… so wonderful. And yet it was in the midst of this horrifying situation. So surreal. And, she wondered, would it even have happened if she hadn't been in such danger? And what would happen if the danger melted away and she returned to Portland and her previous life? Would this romance survive?

But what if the danger worsened? What if another attack was made against her…and Logan? What if neither of them survived?

Get to work, she sternly told herself. She returned to her dad's chair, reminding herself she had serious research to do if she wanted this to turn out right. Important work that could be the difference between life and death—or, at the very least, jail or freedom. She typed Brock's full name and birth date into the search engine and prepared to dig.

TEN

Logan woke to the sound of someone pacing back and forth nearby. He got up and listened intently. It seemed to be coming from the bear cave. So he went out, knocked on the door and Mallory opened it looking relieved.

"Oh, I'm so glad you're awake. I didn't want to disturb you, but I really need to talk. Did you have a good nap?"

"Yes. I feel like a new man." He sat down on the couch, patting a spot next to him. "Have a seat and tell me what's going on."

"Everything!" She eagerly sat down beside him.

"Okay, then." He suppressed the urge to take her in his arms and kiss her again. He reminded himself that he might've jumped the gun earlier. After all, they lived in two different worlds…not to mention Mallory was a murder suspect. "Sounds like your research was successful," he said. "Why don't you start at the beginning."

"First of all, I spoke to Alex Brewster from *Channel Six News* a few minutes ago. He's one of the few people I can still trust over there. And he had some big news. I was so excited that I thought I'd wake you up when I was talking to him."

"When I'm not at the station I tend to sleep like a log. So what did Alex say?"

"He's been doing research on Kestra's murder, and he

unearthed something interesting from a friend at the coroner's office. It sounds like whoever murdered Kestra was trying to make it look like a suicide."

"A suicide?" Logan frowned. "According to the newspaper the murderer slit her throat."

"Apparently her wrists were cut, too." Mallory grimaced. "To be honest, there was so much blood that night, I didn't see the cuts on her wrists. Not even when I took her pulse."

"I'm sure it was a mess…and you were in shock."

She nodded. "But Alex said that her wrists appeared to have been cut *after* she was dead. Naturally, the coroner thought that was odd."

"Yeah. Why would the murderer bother to do that?"

"I think I know," Mallory exclaimed. "It's because Brock wanted *me* dead—not Kestra. And Brock wanted my death to appear to be suicide. I racked my brain over this, but I think it's to appear I was broken up over him."

"But a slit throat does not look like a suicide."

"I know. All I can figure is that the killer botched it somehow. Think about it, Logan, how could a killer sneak up on someone and slit their wrists without a struggle?" She grimaced to imagine this.

Logan slowly nodded. "I suppose that makes sense. And based on the SUV trying to knock us off the road, this killer doesn't seem like the sharpest crayon in the box."

"Thankfully." She stood up and started pacing again. "I know it sounds farfetched. Even to me."

"Sometimes truth is stranger than fiction." He watched her walking back and forth, frustration following her like a shadow. He wished there was something he could do, a way to bring this to an end.

"And so, as I was researching and finding some interesting things, I decided to email some of my findings to Janice Doyle. It seemed only right that the Portland police have access to the same things I was uncovering. But the response I got from Janice sounded pretty cold and skeptical." She stopped pacing and bit her lip with a troubled expression. "I sure hope Brock's not sweet-talking her. He's really good at that. Particularly with women."

"Hopefully she's smarter than that."

Mallory gathered a small stack of printed pages from the desk. "Anyway, I've managed to collect some interesting information on Brock. Stuff the police should be interested in." She was studying something on the computer screen now.

"So what'd you find?" He went over to peek over her shoulder, but instead of reading the papers or screen, he found himself sniffing her hair. It smelled delicious.

"For starters, I found out that Brock grew up in Idaho. He always tells everyone he's from Southern California. Goes on about UCLA. But most of his schooling was in Idaho. He only did one year at UCLA."

"Uh-huh." Logan took one last whiff then stepped away. "Interesting, but doesn't make him a murderer."

"No. Just a liar." She held up another piece of paper. "This is the last thing I found. When Brock was a student at Boise State, during his last year there, a girl named Amanda Samuels went missing."

"And…?" Logan wasn't quite getting the connection.

"Amanda was Brock's girlfriend."

"Oh?" Logan looked down at the page in her hand.

"There are a lot of articles and photos and stuff. At first they thought she'd left of her own volition. But more investigation revealed it was an abduction. And from what I found, Brock was never a suspect. Instead he comes across as the brokenhearted boyfriend, leading searches, putting up posters… It was like it launched him into a campus celebrity."

"Did they ever find the missing girl?"

Mallory shook her head. "No...unfortunately, she's never been heard of since. The assumption is she's dead."

"No body...no suspect...no murder investigation."

"Brock left Boise State the next year. Transferred to UCLA. Probably so he could claim alumni status with what he figured was a more impressive school. He interned with a news show in LA. Looked like he was making a name for himself, a rising star. But from what little I could find, there was some kind of trouble in the workplace and he was let go."

"Let me guess, did the trouble involve a woman?"

"I don't know for sure yet. But I left a message with a receptionist, told her I was an investigative reporter doing a story on Brock, which is actually true, because when I find out the truth I do plan to go public. Anyway, I asked for someone to call—" She stopped talking because her phone jingled. "It's a text," she told him as she looked at her phone. "From 'unknown.'"

"What's it say?"

Mallory looked up at him with frightened eyes. "'When the sun goes down, you're going down, too.'"

He stared down at the words. "Guess that's a warning, huh?"

"It has to mean that the thug in custody wasn't working alone." Mallory pointed at the guns still arrayed on the coffee table. "Ready to do some target practice?"

He considered this. On one hand, he wouldn't mind being outside with an AR-15, ready to take out the creep that wanted to hurt Mallory. On the other hand, he knew better. "I'm not sure I like the idea of you being outside, Mallory. I won't do anything to put you in harm's way."

"But there'd be two of us and we'd be armed," she pointed out with what seemed false bravado.

"Mr. Unknown might be out there and armed, too." Just then the doorbell rang and they both jumped.

"I doubt the killer would ring the doorbell," Mallory said lightly, but her forehead was creased with worry.

"Even so, we'll proceed with caution." Logan picked up the handgun and quickly loaded it. Following his lead, Mallory got her pistol and a handful of bullets. Inserting a couple into the cylinder, she dropped the rest into her pocket, hurrying to catch up with Logan.

He was peeking past the edge of the closed drapes, out the living room window. "It's just Trent Fallows," Logan told her as the doorbell continued to ring. "Probably here to poke around the arson site some more."

"Hey, isn't that Winnie out in the driveway?"

"Looks like it. Maybe she volunteered to assist." Logan unlocked and opened the door.

"About time someone answered. What're you kids up to in there?" Trent peered over Logan's shoulder with way too much interest. "Got something to hide?"

Logan didn't like Trent's tone, but maintained an impassive face. "Sorry to keep you waiting. What's up?"

"Well, you probably heard that we took in the guy driving the SUV that allegedly bumped into you."

"Allegedly?" Logan peered curiously at Trent then decided to soften his approach. "Anyway…I heard he had some contraband, too."

Trent frowned. "Well, that may or may not be true. But I'd like to get some photos of your Jeep. You know, where he hit you."

"There's some black paint on the fender dent, but thanks to my hefty bumper, there's not too much damage." Logan chuckled. "I suspect it hurt the SUV more."

Trent nodded. "Yeah, there was some damage."

"So you're not going to reveal what kind of contraband you found?" Logan pulled out his phone. "I can find out easily enough. Or Mallory's dad can. He's on his way home."

"Maybe you should ask Mallory what the guy had on him." Trent narrowed his eyes. "Sounds like she might know."

"That's ridiculous. I can't believe you'd fall for something like that."

"I could say the same for you. But then it looks like you and Miss Myers have hit it off real nice." Trent pointed to the gun in Logan's hand. "What do you plan to do with that?"

"Just being careful. There's someone dangerous out there."

Trent scowled. "Well, you kids better be careful with those firearms. People who don't know their way around guns can get hurt."

"No worries." Logan kept his voice easy, determined not to react. It would do no good to alienate Trent further. "Feel free to take as many photos of Jeep as you need. I thought maybe you were here to check out the burn site."

"Yeah, I plan on doing that, too. But hearing that you guys running around with guns, I'm glad we made our presence known." He shook a finger at him. "Better be careful where you shoot."

"Don't worry." Logan started to close the door, but Trent stuck his big-booted foot in the way.

"I plan to stick around for a while. Got a lot of looking around to do. And I got copies of your report from the firehouse." Trent jerked his thumb over his shoulder. "Winnie offered to show me around."

"I can walk you through the site if you want," Logan offered.

"I've got Winnie to help. We've got it covered." Trent pulled his foot back.

Logan wanted to argue this point. Winnie hadn't even been part of the investigative team. Logan could show Trent exactly where the incendiary device had been thrown, the angle it seemed to have come from and several other things. But since Trent was determined to play Deputy Know-it-all, why not let him? After all, the information was there in the report. And, if necessary, they could call in more experts on Monday. "Well, have at it." Logan closed the door and shook his head. What an arrogant jerk.

"So, Winnie is helping him?" Mallory looked confused. "Is that normal?"

"It's a small town. Normal is whatever happens."

Mallory held up her revolver. "So, should we do it? Go out and get some target practice? There's a small clearing out back that's good for shooting. And my dad always has a box of old cans and plastic jugs in the garage, ready to use as targets."

Logan considered this. "I appreciate your bravery, but I don't want you out in the open, Mallory. What if someone decides to take a potshot at you?"

"It's pretty wooded all around there. They'd have to move in pretty close to get a clear—" She paused to reach for her jingling phone. "Another text," she said grimly.

"What's it say?"

"'Feeling safe now? Wait until dark.'" She looked around the living room with worried eyes. "Do you think someone's listening to us in here? How do they know we're feeling safe?"

"Are we?"

She frowned. "Not anymore."

"Well, there's no way anyone can hear us in here."

"What about Trent? You told him we were—"

"I'll admit he's a jerk, but I don't really think Trent's in cahoots with criminals."

"Then what does *wait until dark* mean?" She was pacing back and forth again, shaking her phone. "Do you think it's from Brock, threatening from far away? Or does the guy in jail have a friend?"

"I don't know. But I do know this—someone is definitely trying to rattle us." Logan took in a deep breath. "Good reason to stay calm and think clearly."

She stopped pacing and nodded. "Sorry. It just caught me off guard. I was actually starting to feel like we had a little control."

"It's a good warning to be even more careful. No going outside, Mallory." He peered out the slit in the drapes over the front window, trying to see where Trent and Winnie were—wondering if it was possible that Trent actually had sent that text. Although that made no sense.

Mallory stood behind him. "Does it bother you that one of your crew—I mean Winnie—seems to be aligning herself with Trent?"

The truth was, it did bother him. But he knew that was the wrong answer. "Trent is a deputy. He's doing an arson investigation. He probably asked the firefighters for a volunteer. Winnie is always eager to get involved in something exciting. Obviously, she gets a little too involved at times, and the girl needs to watch a little less CSI. But for the most part she's well meaning and energetic…a hard worker."

Mallory just nodded. "So we can trust her?"

"Of course."

"And Trent?"

Logan scratched his head.

"Dad said not to trust him."

"Yeah." Logan nodded. "I agree. But we need to act like we do trust him or it will get worse. And, as fire chief, it's important that I get along with the sheriff's department in order to serve the community, but that's as far as it goes as far as Trent is concerned." He peered out again. "And the truth is, it does bug me that Winnie offered to help him. I'm tempted to march out there and have a talk with her right now."

"Don't hold back on my account."

Logan pressed his lips together, trying to decide. "Okay. Let's make a deal, Mal. I want you to stay in here and start getting all the blinds and drapes closed. This house has a lot of windows, and I don't want us sitting here in a fishbowl. You take care of that, and I'll go have a word with Winnie."

Mallory gave a mock salute. "You got it, Chief."

Logan knew he was probably on a fool's errand as he walked down the graveled driveway. Winnie had already expressed her concern over him being involved with Mallory. It seemed unlikely she'd take him too seriously now. Except that he knew she had a bit of a crush on him. Maybe he could work that angle. Mostly he didn't want Winnie to get hurt. He didn't want anyone to get hurt. Not even Trent.

"Hey," he called out as he approached Winnie. She was on one side of the burned clearing and Trent was on the other, with his back to them.

"Hey, Logan," Winnie said in a friendly tone. "Tired of hanging with a murderer yet?"

He forced a weary smile. "You're only revealing that you're misinformed by saying that, Winnie."

She put her face close to his, staring intensely. "*Really?* I thought you were the misinformed one, Logan. Seriously, what's wrong with you? Aligning yourself with someone like Mallory Myers? Did you even read the newspaper article? What are you thinking?" She narrowed her eyes. "I know about the guy they took in. He's connected to Mallory, Logan. Did you know that?"

"I do know that you don't have all the facts, Winnie."

"And you do?"

"I have a whole lot more than you. You don't know what you don't know, Winnie." Logan didn't want to argue with her. That would accomplish nothing. And now Trent had turned around, so Logan knew he had to talk fast. "Look, Winnie. This situation isn't what you think it is. Mallory is in real danger. There's already been more than one attempt on her life. For all we know there could be another one right here on this property. She's received numerous threats today. And Mallory's best friend was *accidentally* murdered—the hit man mistook Kestra for Mallory. For all we know the killer could mistake you for Mallory next time. You really want to take that risk?"

Winnie looked genuinely alarmed and he thought he was getting through to her.

"Winnie." He placed a hand on her shoulder. "You're part of my crew, and I believe you could be in real danger. I know you're trying to be helpful by volunteering, but I'd feel a lot better if you were back at the station. Okay?"

She blinked in surprise. "Really?"

"What's going on here?" Trent demanded.

"What's going on is I don't like seeing one of my fire-fighters placed in undue danger."

"Danger?" Trent laughed and looked around. "What do you think is going to happen out here?"

"Brock Dennison's lackey might mistake Winnie for Mallory."

"Brock Dennison?"

Logan shrugged.

"You think he's involved in this?" Trent's pale brows arched. "Seriously, you don't believe *that*, do you?"

Logan didn't respond, just watched Trent, trying to gauge his role in this. How much did he know? Why was he so interested?

"Brock Dennison is a respected newscaster," Trent told him. "You honestly think he'd hire a hit man? Or maybe you think Brock's in the mafia now. Come on, Logan, get real. Can't you see this girl is playing you? She wants you to think Brock's the bad guy here, just another smoke screen. Kinda like setting this fire last night."

Ignoring him, Logan turned back to Winnie. "Can't you

see something's going on here?" he asked her. "For your own safety, you need to—"

"Are you kidding?" Trent interrupted. "She's a fire-fighter. A tough girl." He poked Winnie in the arm. "You afraid of something?"

"No way," she retorted.

"I don't know if you understand what's going on," Logan told Trent. "That Mallory is receiving threats on her life. Or that her friend was killed in her place. It's possible that there's a hit man somewhere nearby right now."

"Wow, this girl is really getting to you, isn't she?" Trent chuckled. "You got it bad, man. You're just eating up everything she tosses at you."

"I know what I know," Logan declared. "I just wanted to warn Winnie since she's part of my crew and I don't want her to get hurt." He turned back to her. "I'm not kidding, Winnie. You need to get out of here. Want me to call one of the guys to come pick you up?" He glanced over his shoulder. "You could come in the house to wait until they get here."

"You thought that was safe, but now you're acting like Winnie is in danger by being out here?"

"We changed our minds after Mallory got another text message."

"What kind of message?"

Logan considered how much he wanted to say. "A threat. Not the first one, either."

"If she's getting threats, why doesn't she report them to the sheriff's department?"

"Because she sends them to a Portland detective who's working on the case."

"So, where will you be tonight?" Trent's tone was challenging.

"We'll be staying in the house."

"Fine. Why don't you do that?" Trent turned away.

"Winnie?" Logan tried one last time. "You coming?"

"Hey, I appreciate the concern, but I'm fine. And it's fun working on an arson case that's not just adolescent pranksters. No worries, Logan. I'm a big girl." She gave him a grin.

He slowly shook his head, looking all around him as he walked back to the house. And, sure, he couldn't see any sign of hit men or lowlifes or even a cantankerous squirrel around. No mysterious cars on the road. No unexplained shadows lurking in the trees. But if this thug knew what he was doing, he would probably know how to stay out of sight. At least until dark. Maybe Winnie was safe until then.

"Would she listen?" Mallory asked as he came back inside, pausing to lock the dead bolt behind him.

"Nope. I really tried, too. That girl is stubborn."

"Maybe there's romance in the air—I mean between her and Trent."

Logan chuckled. "Maybe. Although, to be honest, Winnie is usually throwing her romantic whims in my direction."

Mallory's brows shot up. "And do you throw them back?"

"No."

Mallory looked slightly dubious. "She's a pretty girl, Logan."

"I'm sure she's some guy's type."

"Not yours?"

"Not in the least." He frowned. "But I still feel protective of her." He reached for his phone now. "In fact, I think I'll let my assistant chief know that she might be in danger out here. Rod's in charge right now, and he can make an executive decision to insist she return to the station."

It took a little convincing, but eventually Rod agreed to Logan's suggestion, promising to send someone out to fetch Winnie within the hour. Logan felt a small measure of relief as he closed his phone. Still, he wondered, what would be in store for them later tonight? After dark?

ELEVEN

"I thought I'd get some sense of comfort seeing Brock on the *Channel Six News*," Mallory told Logan during the commercial break. They had been preparing dinner as they watched the news from the big-screen TV in the great room, but after twenty minutes Mallory had turned it off. "But I was wrong. Hearing his voice makes my skin crawl." She continued slicing tomatoes for the green salad.

"Comfort?" Logan slid the steaks under the broiler.

"Comfort because, in my mind, he's the one who killed Kestra and my greatest fear was that he was going to kill me, but he obviously couldn't kill anyone while doing live on TV."

"Obviously."

"Doing the news is the perfect alibi for murder. In fact, I suddenly feel certain he'll try to have me killed while he's on the air. I wish we hadn't tuned in at all," she said with remorse. "I should've known he'd lead with Kestra's murder story. It's the big news item of the week. But I never dreamed he'd let Abby Kingston interview him like that. And, if you ask me, it was scripted. I'm sure I could see his eyes reading the teleprompter."

"I thought he seemed surprisingly sincere. And you have to admit that appearing candid was effective."

"I have to admit it made me feel sick," she shot back.

"To hear him pretending to be so distraught over Kestra's death, like he'd lost his one and only true love, when I know for a fact he was using her to get to me. Then acting like he's bending over backward to assist the police to find the murderer. Begging viewers to share information and offering a reward from his own pocket."

"Well, maybe someone out there knows the guy who killed Kestra. Maybe they'll call."

Mallory let out a *humph* noise. "How about him describing his sleepless nights. Yeah, right. And did you notice those dark shadows beneath his eyes?"

"Now that you mention it, yeah."

"It's makeup!" She gave the red onion a loud whack with the chef's knife.

"How could you tell?"

"Because if Brock really had dark circles, Su Jin in makeup would've concealed them completely. And I've seen Brock tired before, like after the all-night telethon, but I've never seen dark circles. Even without makeup, they wouldn't show up beneath his tan. Did you know he uses a tanning bed? No, of course, not. No one knows."

Logan looked slightly uneasy, but Mallory was fired up now, unable to stop. It felt as though all the anxiety that had been penned up inside of her was unleashing. And even though she knew it was ugly and bitter and pathetic, she was unable to stop herself.

"He should get an Emmy for when he said he didn't really think I could've committed the murder, acting all concerned over my reputation and the recent media attack. He almost had me believing him—for a few seconds. But then he comes back with that line about how jealousy does strange things to people, even using the woman scorned quote, but with such sadness and regret. What a jerk!" Mallory threw the chopped onions into the bowl then grabbed a green pepper. "It's like he'd carefully rehearsed every word of it." Mallory whacked the pepper in two. "He says just enough to sound sympathetic about me and then, bam, he throws me under the bus."

Logan folded his arms over his chest as he watched her. "I have to admit this guy is convincing. He really knows his stuff."

"He's a big phony! Can't you see that?"

"Unless he's innocent."

Mallory paused with the chef's knife in mid stroke. "Are you kidding?"

He held up his hands. "Hey, don't brandish that thing at me."

"Seriously?" She waved the knife in the air. "Are you *afraid* of me? You really think I murdered my best friend?"

He turned to open the oven door, taking his time to check on the steaks before he turned around to face her. "No, Mallory, I'm not afraid of you." He dropped the potholder and came over to where she was working. Without saying another word, he slipped an arm around her waist and gave her a gentle squeeze, pulling her close.

"I know, I know," she lowered her voice. "I'm losing it. Letting him get to me again." She paused to absorb the sensation of his arm around her waist. It felt like a cool shower over a smoldering fire.

"It's understandable."

"But useless." It was nice. His arms around her seemed to smooth it all out, as though suddenly Brock hardly mattered.

"Maybe we shouldn't have watched the news." He kissed her on the forehead then stepped away and, folding his arms across his front, leaned against the counter with a hard-to-read expression.

"But seriously," she continued in a calmer voice, "are you buying into Brock's innocence? Just because he's so good on the air? Does it make you believe he's not really behind Kestra's murder? Or last night's fire?"

"I hate to admit it, but this guy comes across as fairly sincere on the screen."

"Yeah, I'm sure that's what all the viewers are thinking. Besides that, he's handsome and charming—how could someone like that be behind such a ghastly crime?"

"If Brock loses his newscaster job, he could go into acting," he joked.

She frowned.

"Want to catch him on the eleven o'clock news, too?" His eyes twinkled in a mischievous way.

"You beast!" She threw a dishtowel at him.

"I was kidding, but come to think of it, it's not a bad idea." He hung the towel by the sink. "For one thing, it would ensure he's still in Portland. And if you're right, if he's really sent someone over here…to get you…well, it's possible that he will slip up on the air."

"Slip up?"

"I don't mean by saying anything. But it'd be interesting to see if his facial expressions change at all. We could study his eyes and see if they reveal anything. At the very least we should record the news show to study later."

"I'm sure he'll be as cool as this." She shook a cucumber at Logan. "Believe me, that man has a heart of stone."

"Speaking of coldhearted men, Rod called me from the station while you were in the bathroom. Apparently Trent threw a hissy fit when they came for Winnie. Even when another firefighter offered to stay in her place, Trent was not having it."

"But Winnie did leave?"

"She did. Fortunately her shift was over and she had plans this evening, anyway. Otherwise, she'd probably still be here."

"And he's still out there?"

Logan peered between the blinds on the kitchen window. "Yep. Still walking around like he expects to make some big discovery. But I'm kinda hoping he stays a while. Having a patrol car parked in the driveway is a nice deterrent to crime, don't you think?"

"Unless the cop is a crook." She put the last cucumber slices on top of the salad then pushed the bowl away. "And I really think he is."

"We need to remember that's a possibility." Logan frowned. "Trent's not real popular with much of anyone in this town. I don't get why Winnie is suddenly a fan."

Mallory slapped her forehead. "That reminds me. I'd meant to do some research on Trent. How long till the steaks are done?"

"Ten minutes, maybe."

She took off down the hall with Logan trailing behind her.

"What're you looking for?" Logan asked as they went into her father's office.

"I'm curious about something." She slid into the chair and the computer screen came to life. "This shouldn't take long."

Logan sank down onto the couch to wait.

"Bingo!" she exclaimed after a couple of minutes.

"What is it?"

"Trent Fallows graduated from Boise State in 2009. That means he was there while Brock was there."

"Do you think they knew each other?"

"It seems possible. I know when I asked Trent about whether he knew Brock, I got a funny reaction from him. It made me suspicious."

"You think Trent's in cahoots with Brock?" Logan lifted the bottom of a blind to peer out the high window.

"I know it seems a long shot, but I have a weird feeling there's a connection. It would explain why he's sympathetic to Brock." Mallory turned off the screen and stood. "We know for certain he's not sympathetic toward me. Even when I tried to be friendly today, he treated me like something stuck to the bottom of his shoe."

"The puzzle pieces fitting together." Logan looked at his watch. "Ready to eat?"

"On one condition." Mallory held up a finger. "Do not let me talk about any of this, okay? Just a nice peaceful dinner."

"Works for me."

It was such a lovely summer evening that Mallory wished they could've eaten outside on the back deck, but knew that wasn't safe. Instead she set the table in the dining room with the good dishes and, even though it was still light outside, with the drapes drawn, it was dark enough to light candles. The effect was lovely. She could almost imagine that they were on a date…a romantic date. Well, except for the firearms laid out across her mom's antique buffet.

With the subject of Brock officially banned, they focused their conversation on each other. They were eager to learn all they could, to fill in the missing blanks. But as they talked about their similar childhoods in the same town, comparing notes about middle school experiences and their favorite teachers in high school, Mallory could almost sense urgency in the air. As if they had to make up for lost time or cram in as much as possible just in case they never got another chance. Even though they weren't talking about what might or might not happen later on, after it got dark, she knew it was on both their minds.

It was close to eight when Logan helped her to rinse the dishes and load the dishwasher, but it was still light outside. For some reason that was reassuring. As she closed the dishwasher, Logan peeked between the wooden slats of blinds above the kitchen sink.

"Is Trent still here?"

"Uh-huh." He let the blind slip back down. "Can't imagine what else he's doing out there. He's got my report. And the area is pretty clean." He rubbed his chin. "Unless…"

"Unless what?"

"Unless he's looking for something specific."

"Like what?" Mallory put the leftover salad in the fridge.

"Well, what if you're right and he's connected to Brock? Is it possible that Brock sent him out here for a purpose? Like, what if that guy in custody really is Brock's lackey and he slipped up? Or maybe he was involved in the fire last night. What if he left something behind that my team missed?"

"But you went over the area pretty carefully, didn't you?"

"Of course, but we were looking for clues related to arson. What if he's looking for something else?"

"Like what?"

"I have no idea, but before it gets dark, I'd like to find out. Plus I want to hear what they found in the SUV today. I'd like to attempt a friendly little conversation with Trent. If that's possible."

"Seriously?" Mallory felt a rush of panic. "Do you think that's wise?"

"Trent is a county deputy," he reminded her. "He reports to Sheriff Lambert, who happens to be a friend of mine. I'm not usually a name dropper, but it might get his attention."

"You're sure about this?"

"We need to determine whether Trent is really the enemy. If he's not connected to Brock, it's an asset to have him around." He placed his hand on her shoulder. "Will you be okay if I leave you alone for a few minutes?"

As Mallory nodded, she wanted to put the kibosh on this, except that his plan made sense. Trent was just one more unknown factor in her already confusing dilemma. "You'll be careful, won't you?"

"I'll be armed with these." Logan patted the pocket that contained his phone then strapped on the shoulder holster and checked the Ruger cylinder for bullets. "I think the handgun is less intimidating than the AR."

Mallory locked eyes with him. "I mean it, Logan. Be really, really careful, okay?" She could feel that shaky feeling coming again, remembering what it was like to be alone and afraid and hopeless. "It's not just that I want you around for protection." She patted his stubbly cheek. "I really kinda like you, too."

Logan slipped the gun into the holster. "I kinda like you, too, Mallory." He gave her a lopsided grin. "More than just kinda." He leaned forward, and for a moment she thought he was about to kiss her again, but instead he kissed her tenderly on the forehead. "Don't forget I'm a fire chief, Mallory. Caution is my middle name."

"Remember what my dad said about Trent." She grabbed her .22 and followed him to the front door. "And if things get dicey, just tell Trent that I'm your backup and that my .22 is loaded and I'm a really good shot."

"Thanks." He peeked out the side window before opening the door. "Make sure you lock up, and if anything goes wrong, call up some of your dad's deputy buddies and tell them to get over here pronto."

After she locked the door, she positioned herself beside the front window with the drapes cracked open just enough for her to peek out. Keeping her eyes pinned on Logan's back as he strolled down the driveway, she felt certain she could defend him if necessary.

TWELVE

Logan kept his stroll easy but confident. He didn't want to intimidate Trent, but he wanted him to know he meant business. "You're still here?" he asked as Trent got out of the patrol car.

"That a problem?"

"Maybe…maybe not." Logan squinted into the sun that was sinking low in the western sky, positioning himself so that it wasn't glaring directly into his eyes.

Trent nodded to the holstered Ruger. "You planning to use that for something?"

"Hope not. But if anyone comes after Mallory, I want to be ready."

"Taking the law into your own hands?" Trent put his hand on his own gun. "Turning vigilante?"

"Self-defense is hardly vigilante." Logan glanced toward the road, trying to see if anyone was parked out there. "What I'd really like to know is what you're doing here, Trent. You're obviously not still investigating the fire."

"I'm on duty."

"You do realize this is private property, don't you?"

"It's also a crime site."

"I'm going to be straight with you, Trent. And I want you to be straight with me. We know for a fact you went to Boise State with Brock Dennison. And we strongly suspect that Brock Dennison is connected to last night's arson as well as the murder of Mallory's friend. What I want to know is just how connected you are to Brock."

"I'm not sure that's any of your business."

Logan pulled out his phone. "Well, it's Sheriff Lambert's business. And he's a good friend of mine—and of Mallory's dad. If he thought you were out here because of a relationship with a possible criminal, a guy who might be guilty of hiring a hit man to murder two innocent young women, I'm pretty certain Gary would want to know."

"So you've really bought into that phony story? I thought you were smarter than that, Logan." Trent's smile looked sleazy. "But I supposed it's easier to swallow baloney when it's coming from a pretty girl."

"Mallory is a news writer, and she knows how to research the facts, Trent. What she's found out about Brock is incriminating and—"

"You honestly expect me to believe Brock Dennison hired a killer to—"

"Do you remember a female student at Boise State? Amanda Samuels?"

"The girl who went missing."

"And you know she was Brock's girlfriend?"

"Sure. Everyone knew that."

"And you know about other women in Brock's life? Ones who've been hurt or gone missing?" Logan knew he was stretching things, fishing a bit, but mostly he wanted to determine Trent's true motives.

Trent frowned. "I've never heard about any other women."

"And yet you're willing to defend Brock? Even though you don't really know about his history with women? Are you saying you'd risk your badge for an abusive—"

"I'm not defending Brock. And before you go off to Sheriff Lambert, you should know that the only reason

I'm out here is because Portland PD asked me to keep an eye on Mallory." He stuck out a defiant chin. "And that's just what I plan to do."

"Is that because you're worried she'll make a run for it? Because I can assure you she won't."

Trent shrugged. "If she does try to run, I'll stop her… or put out an APB and notify State Police and Portland."

"So you really don't believe her?"

He made a smug grin. "Let's just say I have my doubts."

"And that guy that got picked up today. The SUV that ran me off the road. You have any doubts about him?"

"Sure. He's locked up, isn't he?"

"What was in the car, Trent?"

"Evidence."

"Okay, then, tell me the truth, Trent. If someone came around here to hurt Mallory, you'd—"

"I'd do my job," Trent snapped back at him. "I'm here to enforce the law."

"Fine. That's all I wanted to know." Logan stuck out his hand and although Trent hesitated, he shook it. "I'll leave you to it, then." Logan turned around and started back for the house, but as he walked he felt uneasy. Not that he thought Trent was going to shoot him in the back. That was ridiculous. But the sun was getting low and something just didn't feel right. Almost as if he was being watched.

As beautiful as this ponderosa forest was—in daylight— it could feel eerie in the dark. Too many places to hide. Hearing a crunch off to his left, Logan turned, pointing the gun toward the sound and waiting—his heart pounding rapidly as he strained to hear. If it was an animal, wouldn't it keep moving? If it was human—was it watching him?

Keeping his gun pointed toward the source of the sound, and his eyes and ears peeled, he slowly worked his way toward the house. If there was someone out there, maybe it was a good thing they could see this powerful rifle. Maybe it would give them something to think about. That is, unless they were armed with something similar. Or something worse.

He was barely on the front porch when the door swung open and Mallory greeted him with a relieved smile. He hurried inside and, without mentioning the noise, he quickly filled her in on his conversation. "I probably made Trent think we had more dirt on Brock than we really do, just to gauge his reaction."

"And?"

"I really don't think he's working with Brock." Logan sighed. "But I'm not certain. And I wouldn't risk my life—or yours—on that uncertainty."

"And we need to remember what my dad said. We shouldn't trust him."

"I don't. Not completely, anyway. And if he's not working for Brock he'll be a good deterrent for anyone who is. I honestly can't imagine a murderer stepping onto your parents' property with a patrol car parked out front."

"Except that someone was bold enough to come here last night to set that fire. And for all he knew, my dad—a deputy himself—could've been here to apprehend him."

"Good point." He removed the holster, laying it on the kitchen counter. "And don't get me wrong. I do think we need to be on high alert tonight. And I've already started putting together a plan. Want to hear it now?"

"Sure."

"Got any more of that iced tea, first?"

Before long they were back in the bear cave going over Logan's plan. "First of all I need to know if you trust me," he said.

"Of course." She looked slightly offended. "Why wouldn't I?"

"Okay, then, if you don't mind, I'd like to be in command. I know from firefighting how important it is to have one person in charge. When things get dicey and decisions have to be made quickly, you need to know who's calling the shots without any arguments."

"No problem. You can call the shots."

"And you'll do as I say? No questioning me?"

"Absolutely." She smiled. "I trust you, Logan. More than I trust myself in this situation. I remember how petrified I was last night. I couldn't even think straight."

"Okay…good." He took a sip of tea. "For starters, let's go put all the outdoor lights on. You've already got the windows covered as much as possible. But there are some open spots we need to be careful of." As Mallory turned on the lights outside the great room, he noticed how some of the windows in there had no coverings. "And we'll keep all the lights off in here. And when it's really dark, the bear cave is our safe room."

"Sounds good."

"And I think we should put some water bottles and maybe some snacks in there…just in case it's a long night."

"I'll do that."

"And make sure your phone charger's in there." He frowned. "My charger's at home, and my phone's at half now so I'll be leaving it off unless I really need it."

"My dad's got some spare chargers in his office," she told him. "Maybe one will fit."

He set his empty glass in the sink. "Let's round up some flashlights and maybe a camp lantern. And can you find some candles and matches to keep in there? Just in case." He glanced at his watch. "We better get busy. We're burning daylight."

While Mallory gathered the things on her list, Logan went around to be sure all the exterior lights were on and trying to get the lay of the land fixed in his head. Then he searched the garage for a camp lantern, finding a few other things he thought might be handy, as well.

It was dusk when he got back to the bear cave, where Mallory was just setting out some supplies on her dad's desk. He pointed at Mallory's shorts and sandals. "You should probably put on some long pants and sturdy shoes, just in case we need to make a run for it. I doubt that'll happen, but best to be prepared."

"Yeah, I'll do that right now."

Logan peeked out through the wooden blinds, but it was getting too dark to see much, and there was no exterior light to illuminate this side of the house. On one hand, he felt this was the most secure room, but on the other, it offered limited visibility. With the outside light fading fast, it was even darker in here. He decided to light one of the candles Mallory had set on the coffee table. As a firefighter, he was well aware of the dangers of candles, but this one was in a glass jar and looked pretty safe. And the flickering light was cheerful.

Mallory returned wearing jeans, hiking shoes and a plaid flannel shirt. She'd even put her hair into two braids. "How's this?"

"Well, besides being very cute, it looks quite practical." He tugged a pigtail.

"Anything else we need in here?" she asked as she closed the door.

"Not that I can think of." He sat down on the sofa.

She pointed to the glowing candle. "Nice ambiance in the bear cave."

"Smells good, too." He patted the sofa. "Mind if we go over some more plans now?"

She smiled as she sat next to him. "You got it, Chief."

He returned her smile, then turned serious. "So, I'm thinking that if anything goes wrong tonight—like for some reason the house is no longer safe…"

"Why wouldn't the house be safe?"

"Well, it's not exactly a fortress," he pointed out. "Someone who wanted in could break in through a window easily enough." He didn't want to explain how quickly a firefighter could get into a house if necessary. No need to frighten her.

"Oh, yeah." She nodded with worried eyes. "But we'd still be safe in here, wouldn't we? I mean with the dead bolt. We'd be okay for a while. And we've got our guns. Plus we'd call for backup if we heard someone break in. It shouldn't take too long for help to arrive. Deputy Griggs lives over on Corral Road, just five minutes away."

"That's true. But what if there was another fire? We'd have to evacuate."

Her eyes grew wide. "Oh, yeah. I hadn't thought of that. A house fire…that would change things."

"My plan is for us to be prepared for anything and hopefully nothing will happen."

"Right." She nodded.

"So, anyway, should we need to evacuate, we'll head into the woods directly behind your house. I know it'll be too dark to see much out there and it'd be easy to get lost, so my plan is to just find a good spot and wait until reinforcements arrive."

"I know a good place to hide out. There's a wood fort that Austin and I made when we were kids. I think it's still there."

"Can you find it in the dark?"

"Maybe."

"Great. And we'll have our phones so we can communicate with whoever comes out here to help us." He attempted a smile. "If we need it, and really I don't think we will."

"Why wouldn't we just make our getaway in a car?" she asked. "I mean, if we needed to make a run for it."

"I considered that, but if there was really a shooter, a

car would make an easy target. Better to just lie low until help gets here."

"Wow, you've really thought this all out, haven't you?"

He shrugged. "Yeah, I guess. I'd rather be prepared and not need it than the other way around."

"Well, I appreciate—" She paused as her phone jingled. "A text." She looked up with fearful eyes.

"What's it say?"

She peered down at her phone. "'Dark enough for you yet?'"

Logan frowned. "Do you think that could just be Brock, texting from Portland, trying to rattle you?"

"It's working." She dumped her phone on the coffee table as if it was poison, then shuddered. "Why won't he leave me alone?"

"Maybe you're right," he said. "Maybe he's worried you're going to expose his less than lovely past. And if he killed Kestra, the stakes are higher than ever."

She pulled her knees up to her chin and for a moment he could imagine her as a scared little girl…and it got to him. What point was there in scaring her?

"We'll be okay, Mallory." He slipped a comforting arm around her shoulders. "Don't make too much of those texts. That's how a coward fights. And even if he's got a guy out there, the goon might not be any smarter than the guy in lockdown."

"I hope you're right, Logan." Her voice had a slight tremor in it.

"Well, anyway, we're prepared."

"Maybe it's crazy to be here," she said suddenly. "Maybe we should just get out of this house. Before it's too late."

Logan had considered this after his little chat with Trent. Maybe the smart thing would be to hightail it to town. If necessary, they could hang out at the fire station all night, figure something else out in the morning. He got up to peek out the blinds, but it was even darker now than before. "I don't like the idea of us going out there in the open, Mallory. Not in the dark. We'd be sitting ducks in a vehicle."

"Is Trent still here?"

"I can't see in the dark." He wondered about shining a flashlight out the window. Perhaps he could pick up the reflective strip on the cruiser. But the beam of light would draw attention back to them. That might not be good.

"Oh, Logan!" she suddenly exclaimed. "It's a mistake to stay out here all night. I mean it seemed like a good plan earlier...but I'm getting really scared now."

He hated to admit that he agreed with her. He'd tried to downplay the danger today. Partly for Mallory's sake, to reduce her anxiety. But also because her theory had seemed so far-fetched and unlikely. And after the guy in the SUV got picked up, he'd felt the danger was gone.

She picked up her phone again, shaking her head. "I wish there was a response I could send...something to make him think twice."

"Maybe you should write something that expresses confidence," he suggested.

"Okay." Using her thumbs, she talked as she wrote. "Not afraid of dark. Not alone. Prepared for anything. Police backup."

"Yeah," he said eagerly. "That sounds good. No wonder you're a writer. Maybe the pen really is mightier than the sword."

"We'll see." She hit Send, then set her phone down.

"We're going to be okay." He was about to slip his arm around her again, when he heard a loud scream from outside.

Mallory grabbed on to him with a terrified expression. "What was that?"

"It sounded like a woman." He picked up the Ruger holster, quickly strapping it on. Then he picked up the automatic rifle. "I thought Winnie would be gone by now, but it's possible she changed her mind."

"Do you think it's her?"

Logan was already unlocking the door. "I'm going to find out."

THIRTEEN

With her holster on and her rifle in hand, Mallory followed him through the darkened house. She wanted to tell him to stay inside, that it was dangerous out there—that she couldn't bear to see him get hurt, but the shrill sound of another scream froze the words in her throat.

"I'm going out," he said quietly as he slowly opened the door. "You stay here and—"

"I've got your back," she whispered before he could finish. And then she pushed her way out behind him.

"Mallory," he hissed at her. "Stay—" But another scream interrupted him and Mallory spotted what looked like Winnie, facedown in the driveway.

"Look." She pointed across the lawn.

Logan took off and she trailed behind him, but they were only halfway across the lawn when a shot rang out. Logan hit the ground and Mallory, certain he'd been shot, threw herself down beside him. Before she could ask, he grabbed her, pulling her behind one of the tall ponderosa tree trunks as two more shots rang out. "Are you okay?" he asked.

"Yes! And you?"

"Yeah. You have your phone?"

She patted her shirt pocket. "Yeah."

"Call for backup now. And you stay here while I get Winnie. I'm going to drag her behind your car."

"But what if they shoot at you?" She held up her rifle. "Let me back you up. I probably can't hit anyone in the dark, but I can scare them."

"Okay. Just stay in the shadow of the tree. Be safe." Logan took off, and sure enough another shot exploded. Remaining close to the tree, Mallory aimed her rifle toward the sound and returned fire, exchanging two more rounds and praying that Logan had gotten Winnie to safety by now.

Suddenly everything around her was eerily quiet. She strained her ears to listen, trying to determine if the shooter was on the move, but she heard nothing. Rolling back around into the shadow of the tree, she saw that Winnie was no longer lying in the driveway. That was some comfort. But where were they? And how was she supposed to get back into the house without getting shot? And what if Logan had been shot? For all she knew, he could be bleeding to death right now. Should she make a run for it? See if she could help him? But he'd told her to stay put and she'd promised to listen to him. So far she hadn't done too well with that promise.

With her heart pounding hard, she silently prayed for Logan's safety. She knew she'd be devastated if anything had happened to him. And she would blame herself—perhaps even more than she blamed herself for Kestra's death. Why had she allowed Logan to get involved in this mess? Why had she encouraged him to stay out here with her? Isolated like this in the woods? What was she thinking? And would this nightmare ever end?

She looked at the shadow of the tree behind her. A long path of darkness, created by the bright porch light, it ran across the driveway and into the woods back there. She wondered if the shadow could conceal her form as she ran through it. If she could reach the trees alongside the driveway, she might be able to make her way through the woods and around to the back of the house to let herself in.

Except that the house was locked up tight. The only door not locked was the front door. Besides that, she had to find Logan. He might be hurt!

They needed help and they needed it now. She was just reaching for her phone when she heard a rustling sound coming from behind the tree. She knew it couldn't be Logan because he had gone the other direction. Certain it was the shooter, she took off, trying to conceal herself with the shadow of the tree but, as she ran, two more shots blasted through the darkness.

When she reached the edge of the driveway she pulled out her pistol, and although she could see nothing she returned fire. She suspected the shooter was using the big ponderosa trees for cover, just as she was. Although she was concealed in the shadows right now, all around her was the brightly lit area from the oversize garage light that her dad had installed for security. If she left this spot, she'd be clearly visible.

"Mal," Logan called out from the shadowy area on the other side of the garage. "I'm coming to you. Cover me."

She got her rifle ready, aiming it across the front yard to where the shots had come from. As soon as she heard Logan's footsteps she started to shoot, hoping to create a distraction. As expected, her shots were followed by more shots, but Logan made it to her, hunkering with her behind the tree trunk.

"I've got to get to the front door," he said breathlessly. "You send out a couple more shots while I go around the cars." He held up the automatic rifle. "When I'm in the open, running for the door, I'll use this. And that's when I want you to get to the garage side door. That's where Winnie is. I'll run through the house, unlock it and let you guys in. Got it?"

"Got it." She nodded as she pulled out her pistol. She knew her rifle was probably down to one round by now.

"But let me reload first." She grabbed out several of the spare rounds in her pockets, but her hands were so shaky it was difficult and Logan reached over to help her.

"Ready?" Logan looked into her face then leaned forward to kiss her forehead. "Be safe."

"You, too." As he took off, she started shooting toward the trees in the side yard, wishing that the shooter would step out so she could see him. As much as she hated the idea of killing anyone, she thought she could do it if it was to spare Logan. But seeing that Logan was safely behind the cars, she picked up the rifle and prepared herself to make a run for it. As soon as she saw Logan come out from behind her car, shooting the automatic rifle, she made a mad dash for the side of the garage with the rounds of gunfire ringing in her ears. *Please protect him*, she prayed silently as she ran.

She found Winnie on the ground next to the garage side door. "Are you okay?" she whispered breathlessly before she realized the gunfire had ceased.

"Where's Logan?" Winnie said gruffly. "Has he been shot?"

"Shh!" Mallory squatted down by her, trying to listen for footsteps, praying that Logan was inside and not hurt. Suddenly the door next to them burst open and Logan grabbed hold of Winnie. With Mallory's help he dragged her into the garage, then closed and locked the door behind them.

"Are you okay?" Mallory asked him as they all hunkered down together in a corner of the garage.

"Fortunately the maniac out there is no marksman."

"Or else we've just managed to keep him rattled by returning fire," she said.

"Let's get Winnie into the house," Logan said. "But stay down low."

"Was she shot?" Mallory asked as they carried Winnie across the garage.

"No," Winnie declared in an aggravated tone. "*She* fell and hurt her ankle."

Mallory wanted to ask Winnie what she was doing out there in the dark night and why she was screaming like that, but instead paused in the laundry room to lock the garage door behind them. "I haven't had a chance to call for help yet," she told Logan.

"I already called 911," Winnie said. "Trent should be here soon."

"Why isn't Trent out there now?" Mallory asked suspiciously.

"I don't know," Winnie admitted. "I came out here to see him, but his cruiser was gone."

"That figures," Logan said in a terse tone when they got to the living room. "Let's set her down here."

"And I'm calling for backup," Mallory said as she grabbed her phone, hitting the speed dial she'd set up earlier.

"I said I already did that," Winnie told her.

"Yeah, but I'm calling one of my dad's—" She stopped when she heard Stan Griggs barely saying "Hello" and hurried to explain the situation. "Someone already called 911, but no one's here yet. And my dad said to call you."

"I'll be there in five minutes," he told her, "I'll call for more backup on my way. Was anyone hurt? Need an ambulance?"

"Winnie hurt her foot, but no one was shot. Well, unless the shooter took a bullet."

"Do you have a description on the shooter?"

"All I could see was that he had dark clothing."

"Well, I'm already out the door. You kids stay inside and don't take any chances."

"Will do." With trembling hands, she slipped her phone

into her shirt pocket then looked at Logan as she shone a flashlight on Winnie's swollen foot.

"Looks like a sprain," he said in a flat tone. "You'll live." He turned away and went over to a front window, cautiously peering through the crack of the drapes.

"See anything?" Mallory asked.

"No, but I think we should get away from these windows, just in case the shooter decides to take some more pot shots. Never know…he might hit the mark."

Mallory helped Winnie down the hallway. She unlocked the bear cave door and they set Winnie down on the couch.

"I'm sure they'll be here shortly," Logan said as he headed for the door. "You girls stay here and I'll keep a watch out there." And, just like that, he was gone. Mallory opened the ice chest and handed Winnie a chilled bottle of water. "You can use it to ice your ankle or just drink it." She wasn't eager to be locked in here with Winnie, but decided to put on her journalist hat and see if she could get to the bottom of this.

"So you came out here tonight to see Deputy Trent?" Mallory gently probed.

"Yeah. I felt sorry for him, sitting out there all by himself."

"But I thought Logan told you to go home—for safety's sake." She tried not to sound as irritated as she felt. But it seemed that Winnie had put all of them at risk by coming back here. They both could've been killed trying to rescue the foolish girl. For all Mallory knew, they were still in danger.

Winnie twirled a long strand of hair between her fingers, as if thinking hard. "I didn't think there was any real danger," Winnie began slowly.

"But Logan had told you otherwise." Mallory frowned. What kind of firefighter was Winnie if she didn't even listen to the fire chief's orders?

"I know, but I told Trent that I was meeting friends at Papa Mario's tonight, and all he had was a candy bar and soda. So I promised to bring him the leftover pizza."

"You risked everyone's life for pizza?"

Winnie took a sip of water, then shrugged. "I didn't mean to."

"Right…" Mallory suppressed the urge to shake this silly girl. "So Trent wasn't here when you arrived?"

"As far as I could see. The cruiser wasn't around."

"Then why didn't you just leave?" Mallory studied her. She was undeniably spunky, but maybe she lacked good sense. Mallory couldn't quite figure her out.

"That's what I was doing. But the driveway is narrow so I couldn't turn around easily, and I'm not good at backing up. So my car was all sideways and partly off the driveway with my front wheels spinning in the soft dirt."

"Uh-huh?"

"I was looking in the rearview mirror and, in the backup lights, I see this guy running up toward my car. He's dressed in dark clothes and has what looks like an automatic rifle." She shook her head. "I totally freaked. I mean, there I am in my car which is sort of stuck and this guy is running straight for me. I tried gunning my engine which just made a cloud of dust, then I leaped out of my car and took off running for the house."

"Did he shoot at you?"

"No. But I tripped on the edge of the driveway." She leaned down to touch her puffy ankle. "I wonder if it's broken."

"I don't know." Mallory frowned. "I'm surprised the shooter didn't kill you."

"I guess I wasn't the one he was going after."

Mallory shook her head. "Yeah, you don't really look anything like me."

"So, you think he wanted to kill *you*?"

Mallory could hear the sound of sirens now. "That sure took long enough," she said as she peered through the high window. When she turned around, Winnie was crying. "What is it?" Mallory asked. "Are you in pain?"

"I don't know," she sobbed. "I guess it's all just hitting me. I think of myself as a brave person, but I've never been so scared in my life. I didn't know what to do. I wasn't even sure if I could walk after I fell. So I just lay there on the ground. I guess I hoped he'd think I was dead or something. Like playing possum. Truth is, I was too scared to move. And my foot felt like it was on fire." She wiped her nose with her wrist. "I still can hardly believe what happened."

"It was pretty scary."

"Yeah. So there I am, lying on the ground, feeling helpless, and just when I'm thinking the shooter's on his way to finish me off, Logan swoops in and gathers me up like I'm as light as a feather." Her tears seemed to melt into a smile. "He probably saved my life."

Mallory wanted to add that she had been Logan's backup, but thought, *Why bother?*

"There was so many gunshots that I thought for sure someone would be dead," Winnie continued.

"Well, hopefully one of those bullets got the gunman, but I hope he's not dead."

"You're kidding!" Winnie scowled. She pressed the water bottle against her swollen foot. "He's out there shooting at everyone like a maniac. And because of him I got hurt and who knows how long it'll take to heal up so I'll be able to return to work again."

Mallory wanted the gunman to be alive in order to make a confession that would reveal Brock Dennison's involvement in this whole nasty business. Because nothing else made sense. She wanted this criminal, as well as the one in jail, to confess to being Brock's hired thugs and, in all likelihood, responsible for Kestra's death, too. What happened to them after that made no difference to her. She simply wanted Brock to be exposed and brought to justice, and for this madness to end. And then, perhaps, she could return to her old life. Or find a better life.

She was just imagining a happy ending to this frightening story when she heard her phone chiming, signaling that another text had just been received. She wished that it was from Logan or even her dad, confirming that he was on a red-eye, but the sender was, once again, "unknown."

You still there? Still living and breathing? If so, enjoy it while it lasts because it won't be long until it's all over.

Mallory shuddered as she stared at the bold words. Whoever sent them obviously didn't know that the conspiracy to murder her tonight had gone sideways...or had it?

FOURTEEN

Logan regretted leaving Mallory with Winnie. But he knew that, in order to protect them, he needed to follow through with the shooter still outside. Although he hadn't admitted as much, he was relatively certain that he'd seen the shooter fall after one of his shots. But with the two women still locked outside of the garage, there had been no time to investigate. And, although help was coming, he didn't want the gunman to get away.

If the gunman wasn't seriously wounded, he might be more determined than ever to get to Mallory while he still had the chance. So with the fully loaded Ruger in his holster and the automatic rifle in hand, Logan turned off the rear exterior lights then slipped out the back door and, going around the far side of the house, cautiously approached the shadowy front yard where he'd seen the gunman fall.

To his relief that guy was still there. Lying on his side, he was curled up in a fetal position. Not moving. Just the same, Logan was careful on his approach. Creeping up from behind him, Logan grabbed the rifle that the gunman had used, tossing it well out of reach.

"You alive?" Logan asked in a gruff voice. As much as he'd wanted to stop the gunman, his goal had never been to kill him. And even though Logan knew, from taking gun classes, that it was safer to shoot to kill in a self-defense situation, he hoped that this creep was still breathing.

The guy let out a low groan and Logan felt a small wave of relief. Even so, he didn't trust this guy. For all he knew, the gunman could still be armed with a handgun. "Don't move," he told him. "I don't want to have to shoot you again."

The guy just moaned.

"Are you working alone out here? Or is there someone with you?" Logan glanced over both shoulders as he planted a foot on the wounded man's back, ready to shoot, if necessary. When the guy said nothing, Logan nudged him with his foot, eliciting another loud groan. "You working alone, man?" Logan demanded. "Tell me the truth and it will go better for you." He nudged him again. "Hear those sirens in the distance? Medical help is on the way. Tell me, are you working alone?" This time he nudged him quite firmly.

"Alone," the man gasped.

"But Brock Dennison sent you?"

The guy said nothing.

"Answer me!" Logan nudged him again. "How much did Brock pay you?" But the guy was silent now. Logan hoped he wasn't dead. Down the driveway a pair of headlights were quickly approaching. Hopefully they belonged to Deputy Griggs. Not far behind, on down the road, came a short stream of flashing lights and emergency vehicles. Keeping his gun handy, Logan called Griggs's number, informing him of his whereabouts. "I'm in the front yard. With the gunman. He's shot, but still alive."

Deputy Griggs got there quickly and together they rolled the shooter over. Then Griggs frisked him for weapons—securing an additional handgun and a large hunting knife—and finally Griggs handcuffed him and read him his rights.

"He said he's working alone," Logan told Griggs. "But I wouldn't believe him. The other guy—the one who ran me off the road earlier—he's probably connected with this guy. And who knows whether they have any other criminal friends crawling about the woods."

Within minutes, the other emergency vehicles arrived and not long after that, both the shooter and Winnie were being transported to the hospital.

Eager to get back to Mallory, Logan found her still sitting in her dad's office with a very dejected expression.

"You okay?" He leaned down to look into her face. "You heard we got him, didn't you?"

She nodded. "Yeah. And that he's still alive and on the way to the hospital."

"Good news, eh?"

She gave him a weak smile.

"Then why so glum?"

She held up her phone. "This just came…a few minutes ago."

It's not over until it's over. Not until you meet up with Kestra again.

He read the words then shook his head. "It figures. Well, I already decided that we should get out of here for the night." He reached for her hand.

She peered curiously at him. "But Deputy Griggs seemed fairly assured that I'd be safe now that the shooter is in custody."

"Yeah…he's probably right. And Perez appeared to be alone."

"That's his name?" she asked. "Perez?"

"Yeah. Antonio Perez. Ring any bells?"

"No." She shook her head as she slowly stood.

"But even though Perez claims he's on his own, we don't know that for certain."

"Yeah… I guess not."

"The deputies and detectives will do a thorough search over the whole property. Probably late into the night. So it won't be exactly peaceful around here. And until we're a hundred percent positive that Perez didn't have an accomplice, I'd feel better if we stayed someplace else tonight."

She looked slightly relieved. "Yeah, that makes sense."

"Get whatever you need for the night," he said as they walked through the house. While she gathered her things, he looked out the window, watching as flashlight beams moved about through the trees. He knew the deputies were searching for Perez's car. Some of the emergency vehicles still had their flashing red and blue lights running, which added to the drama of the crime scene. Thanks to Winnie's 911 call and Griggs's request for additional help, the place was crawling with law enforcement. If there was another gunman, Logan felt relatively sure he'd be hot-footing it out of here by now. Even so, he didn't want to take any chances. No need to stick around.

As he ushered Mallory out to his Jeep, Logan's eyes roamed from right to left. He knew they weren't out of harm's way yet. "Maybe you should keep low," he said as he started the engine.

"You mean put my head down again?"

"Just in case there's another shooter between here and the main road. It's probably paranoia on my part, but I'd feel better."

She leaned forward, putting her head between her knees. As he backed out, he reached over to pat her on the back. "It won't be for long. I'll let you know as soon as I'm sure the coast is clear."

"Maybe you should put your head down, too."

He smiled. "Hard to drive like that. But I'll go fast." At least that would make them a tougher target, he thought as he stepped on it, going off-road to avoid the other vehicles and making it to the main road with no shots fired.

A mile or so down the road, he told her she could sit up. "Sorry to be overly cautious. But after everything...well, you just never know."

Mallory let out a tired-sounding sigh. "So...where are we going?"

"A safe haven."

"Your place? The fishbowl?"

"My other place. The firehouse."

She chuckled. "Really? They won't mind if I spend the night there?"

"They?" He laughed. "Remember, I'm the chief. And as long as you don't complain about the bunk or the food, I'm pretty sure you'll be welcome."

They rode in silence for a while, but finally Mallory broke it. "Do you think the gunman is going to live?"

"I hope so."

"Really?" she sounded slightly surprised.

"Yeah, sure. Why wouldn't I?"

"Oh... I don't know...something Winnie said."

"What's that?"

"She didn't seem so concerned about him living. I want him to be alive to testify against Brock. I want him to bring the truth to light. Guess that's kind of selfish."

He shrugged. "Well, my reasons for wanting him alive are selfish, too. I just don't like the idea of being responsible for killing a man."

"But it was in self-defense," she argued. "And you were defending Winnie. And me, too."

"That's true. But I didn't really want to kill him."

"And apparently you didn't." She turned to look at him. "Did he say anything—I mean anything about his motive, who he was working for?"

"I tried to get him to talk. Other than claiming to be alone, he was pretty quiet. I mentioned Brock's name, and he never said a word. But I think the silence was telling."

"How's that?"

"He could've denied knowing Brock. But he didn't."

"Will someone question him further at the hospital?"

"Absolutely."

Mallory let out another long sigh, leaning back into the seat. "I called my dad after I heard the gunman was in custody. I wanted to reassure him that I was okay. But he'd already booked a red-eye flight for tomorrow night. He'll arrive really early Sunday morning. But maybe I should tell him to cancel it. Maybe with Perez locked up…maybe he doesn't need to come home, after all."

"I don't know." Logan figured this decision was probably best left to Deputy Myers.

"I made another call, too," she said quietly.

"Uh-huh?"

"To my friend Alex." Her tone had a mysterious edge to it.

"Alex?"

"Remember my friend in the newsroom? He's a writer for *Channel Six*, too."

"Oh, yeah. So what did you tell Alex?"

"I gave him an anonymous tip."

"Anonymous?"

"Well, I asked him to keep it anonymous, and he promised he would."

"What was your tip?" Logan was pretty sure he knew, but what he didn't know was—*why*? Why would Mallory want to poke what could turn out to be a hornet's nest? It seemed more prudent to simply lie low…for the time being.

"I told him about the gunman. About how he had tried to kill us—and that he was hospitalized. I also mentioned that he was on my parents' property and was possibly linked to arson the night before."

"What did Alex say about that?"

"Naturally, he was very interested. He promised to look into it right away."

"And you really think you can trust this guy…this Alex?"

"I hope so. Like I told you before, he's not a fan of Brock Dennison."

"Ah…"

"The big question was whether they can run it as a story tonight or not. Alex wasn't sure he could get it all together in time for the late broadcast. But he promised to write it for the co-anchor—Abby Kingston. I didn't want Brock to get his hands on it."

"Well, even if it can't be on tonight's news, at least he's working on it." Logan let out a tired yawn as he turned down the street to the firehouse.

"You must be exhausted," Mallory said in an apologetic tone. "And all because of me."

"I'm a little tired." He tried to sound light. "Nothing a good night's sleep can't fix."

"I'm sorry that I dragged you into my problems," she said quietly. "This was supposed to be your time off and—"

"Hey, don't misunderstand me, Mallory. I was happy to spend the evening with you. I knew exactly what I was getting into, and I'd do it all over again in a heartbeat."

"I really appreciate it, Logan." Her voice sounded shaky. "I honestly don't know what I'd have done without you." She held up her hands. "I might be dead."

A cold chill ran through him. She was probably right—she very likely would be dead. And then what would he do? "What time is it?" He saw the firehouse ahead.

"Almost eleven."

"Want to watch the eleven o'clock news?" He parked in the side lot.

She didn't answer right away.

"Or if you'd rather not—"

"No," she said firmly. "It should be very interesting. And informative."

The bright lights of the firehouse felt like a warm welcome to him. Such a different world than the one they'd just left. "Our safe haven," he announced as turned off the engine. "For tonight, anyway."

"I really appreciate it."

As he led her inside, he knew he'd have to more fully explain tonight's strange situation to his crew. Because the paramedics had been first responders, everyone here would already know about Winnie's accident, but details regarding the gunman would probably be sketchy. So, while Mallory took a seat on the sagging sofa, he attempted to enlighten his buddies on the interesting events of the evening.

"So Winnie's at St. John's, getting some X-rays and whatever, but I'm sure she'll be just fine." He grabbed the remote and tuned the TV to the Portland news channel. "The gunman, who may also be the perpetrator in last night's arson, is in custody. He's also at St. John's."

As the news show's theme music began to play, Logan went over to his usual chair, an old recliner his mom had donated to the firehouse, and eased himself down. He felt tired to the bone and hoped he didn't doze off before the news show was finished. "And now, if you don't mind, Mallory and I want to watch this." He put his feet up. "It's possible that the news anchor is involved with these crimes."

"You don't mean Brock Dennison?" a female firefighter named Jennifer asked him.

Logan just nodded.

"You're saying Dennison is involved with your gunman and in Winnie getting hurt?" TJ asked.

"Possibly." Logan turned up the volume.

"You gotta be kidding." TJ looked skeptical.

"Time'll tell." Logan hoped he hadn't said too much.

"No way," Jennifer declared. "Brock Dennison is a good guy. He's always working on benefits for kids and stuff. No way could that guy be a criminal. That's just crazy."

Logan simply shrugged, but Mallory looked decidedly

uneasy as she grabbed a throw cushion and clutched it to her chest. Did she regret coming here with him now? As the news show started the firefighters began to chat amongst themselves and Logan had to give them a shush signal.

"Seriously, folks, we want to watch this. Go somewhere else if you need to yack."

The room got quiet as the newscasters started sharing news highlights from the day, but apparently Portland was having a rather quiet summer evening because most of the stories were pretty ho-hum. In fact, it was so boring that Logan knew it should be putting him to sleep, but something about Brock Dennison's smug tanned face made Logan feel wide-awake. If that pretty boy was truly behind all this nastiness, Logan would enjoy the chance to wipe that smile off his face. The monster had to be stopped.

FIFTEEN

Mallory felt her stomach twist into a knot as Brock's tanned face filled the big-screen TV. How had she ever thought him attractive? Right now he looked like evil in a fancy facade. She wondered that others couldn't see it, too. As he attempted some light humor about a dog event taking place at the River Park on Saturday, she wanted to scream—*can't you all see this man is a murderer?* Instead, she pressed her lips together and hugged the throw cushion even more tightly to her chest. It would do no good for all for Logan's firefighter friends to see her acting like a crazy woman. For his sake, she needed to keep herself together.

To her relief, Abby Kingston's pretty face replaced Brock's. She'd never been a huge Abby fan, but compared to Brock, this woman felt like a breath of fresh air. "We've got breaking news coming from the other side of the mountain tonight," Abby said suddenly. "It seems that in the small town of Clover, just three hours from Portland, there's been a shooting incident. It happened earlier this evening and facts are still coming in, but at this time we know two people were hurt."

The firehouse got very quiet now—and Mallory's full attention was on the screen where a photo of downtown Clover was being shown. She knew this was the story derived from the tip she'd given Alex. Bless him for throwing it together so quickly. The camera returned to Abby Kingston as she described the sleepy little town. But suddenly Mallory wished it would pull back to show Brock, as well. She longed to see his reaction when he heard that his nasty plans had gone awry.

"In tonight's skirmish a local firefighter—a young woman named Winnie Halston—was injured in a shoot-out that involved a Portland man named Antonio Perez. Details of Ms. Halston's injuries are sketchy, but sources say that Perez suffered a gunshot wound that is not life threatening. He's listed in serious condition. And both are hospitalized in a local facility. Authorities say that Perez is also a suspect in an arson incident that occurred the previous night.

"According to our sources, Perez may also become a suspect in a recent Portland murder case. Kestra Williams was brutally slain in Portland just last Wednesday. This unsolved case is of special interest to this particular news station because the apartment where Williams was murdered belongs to one of our own news writers. Mallory Myers, on temporary leave of absence, was considered a suspect in the Williams murder case early on and continues to be of interest. What possibly links these crimes together is that tonight's shootings occurred on a rural piece of property owned by Ms. Myers's parents." She paused, turning to Brock. "The plot thickens."

Without missing a beat, Brock jumped in. "On the topic of the Williams murder case, police authorities have revealed that the article of clothing used to cover the surveillance camera at Mallory Myers's apartment did, in fact, belong to Ms. Myers." Now a picture of a Blazers T-shirt was shown on the screen. And although Mallory had owned a T-shirt similar to that, she felt certain it wasn't the same shirt and that this was simply a shirt the news team had borrowed for this piece.

"Authorities are currently investigating whether anyone

suspicious was spotted at the time the surveillance cam was obscured," Abby added.

"I know for a fact that the security cam is located in a place where few people can see it," Brock said. "And it was obstructed shortly before Ms. Williams was murdered in Myers's apartment, a little while before Ms. Myers came home."

"That sure doesn't bode well for Mallory Myers." Abby sounded worried.

"I still have difficulty believing that Ms. Myers could be responsible for such a heinous crime." Brock's forehead creased. "But this breaking news—tonight's shootings, and on the Myers' property—well, it does seem to cast additional suspicion on our young news writer." He grimly shook his head. "It certainly does not look good."

"Very sad," Abby added.

Brock looked directly into the camera. "Our hearts go out to Kestra Williams's family and friends. They have asked that we keep them in our prayers. Ms. Williams's memorial service is scheduled for tomorrow afternoon." He turned to Abby with a very somber expression. "I've been asked by the family to deliver her eulogy." He let out a sad-sounding sigh. "I am honored by this invitation, and it was with great sadness that I accepted. Tomorrow is going to be rough."

Abby reached over to pat Brock's hand. "I'm so sorry for your loss, too, Brock. I know Ms. Williams was a close personal friend."

He just nodded. "And now for weather. Candy Bowman, what can we expect for our upcoming weekend? Hopefully not another scorcher."

Mallory quickly stood and, without saying a word, hurried from the overly warm and crowded room. She needed air and she needed it now. Finding the nearest exit, she burst out of the firehouse and into the cool night air. Just seeing and hearing Brock made her feel sick to her stomach.

"You okay?"

She turned in surprise to see Logan had followed her out. "I—uh—I don't know."

"That was pretty rough."

"I cannot believe Brock!" she exclaimed. "It's like he's out to get me on every level. He doesn't just want me dead and buried, he wants to completely smear my reputation, too."

"And he does it so innocently."

Mallory did not appreciate that comment—even if it was true—but decided to keep her thoughts to herself.

"What about that surveillance cam?" Logan asked. "Was that really your shirt?"

"Apparently." She pressed her lips together.

"Are there other security cameras?"

"My apartment is in an old house that was remodeled into four apartments. Just the one cam. Out by the alley."

"Interesting that Brock was aware of it."

"We used to date. Remember? It's no secret." She let out a weary sigh. "I'm really tired. I'm sure you are, too."

"Yeah. How about I direct you to the women's quarters? I asked someone to put your bag in there for you."

"Thanks."

As they went back into the firehouse, Logan pointed out some of the highlights and told her to help herself to the kitchen where a couple of men were having a late-night snack. But Mallory was not eager to engage with any of the other firefighters. She could only imagine what they were thinking of her after that newscast. Why had she even wanted to see it? She wondered if Logan had spoken in her defense after she'd run off. Perhaps there hadn't been time. And maybe she didn't really care. As he pointed her toward a door, all she felt was tired and beat up...and slightly hopeless. Even so, she forced a small smile. "Thank you," she murmured. "For everything."

He placed a hand on her shoulder. "Sleep well."

"You, too."

Mallory went into the room where two sets of bunk beds were against the walls, but none of the bunks were occupied and the lights were still on. Her bag was on one of the lower bunks and she assumed that was where she was supposed to sleep. She was just heading toward it when a blonde woman dressed in a uniform emerged from what appeared to be the bathroom.

"Oh, it's you," she said as she kicked off her shoes.

"Have we met?" Mallory couldn't remember the woman's name, or if she was even the same woman in the TV room earlier.

"Not officially." The woman unbuttoned her shirt.

"I'm Mallory." She attempted a friendly smile. "I actually grew up in Clover. My dad's a deputy and—"

"Yeah, I know who you are." The woman seemed to be studying her closely. "I'm Jennifer...and Winnie is a good friend of mine."

"Oh, yeah, of course." Mallory nodded. "That was too bad... I mean her getting hurt. But like Logan said, she was fortunate. She could've been killed by Perez. Any of us could've been killed."

"Like your friend in Portland?" Jennifer's eyes narrowed with what seemed suspicion.

Mallory frowned. "Well, I don't know. I mean, that was different."

"How so?" Wearing a tank top and uniform pants, Jennifer sat down on a lower bunk, folding her arms across her front.

"Well, Kestra was, uh, she was murdered with a knife." Mallory shuddered to remember. "Tonight the killer was armed with a gun."

Jennifer tipped her head to one side. "I guess I should be feeling pretty scared."

"Scared? Why?"

"It seems that wherever you go trouble follows. A girl gets killed. Another one gets hurt. And then there's that fire. Here you are with me—should I be worried?"

Mallory didn't know what to say...what to do. Mostly she wanted to just run...but where? A large hard lump was growing in her throat. But she was determined not to cry.

"Seriously, doesn't it seem a little strange to you?"

"Yeah...it is strange." Mallory's voice grew gruff as she tried to hold back tears.

"I mean, even the newscasters are acting like you're suspicious. If you ask me, it's pretty weird. And then Logan insinuates that Brock Dennison is somehow involved in all this. But *you* saw him on the news tonight—how could he possibly be part of these crimes? He's hours away. It makes no sense to me."

"I'm sure it doesn't." Mallory looked toward the door, wanting to leave—to go anywhere to get away from this heartless young woman.

"But Logan seems to believe you." Jennifer stood up and, coming closer, she peered curiously at Mallory. "And he must think that you're not dangerous, otherwise he wouldn't have brought you here."

"I can see that my presence makes you uncomfortable." Mallory picked up her bag. "Please, excuse me." And before Jennifer could say another word, Mallory exited the room. And without speaking to anyone, she left the building. She had no plan...no place to go. And her car was still parked at her parents' house. She glanced up and down the dark and deserted street and was slightly surprised to realize that she didn't feel the least bit afraid. Perhaps it was because she was too numb to feel anything. Or maybe she had quit caring.

Looping the handle of her bag over her shoulder, she began to walk toward the center of town. She felt slightly guilty about leaving like this—but she also knew it would've been impossible to stay. Hopefully Logan was fast asleep by now. She would send him a text in the morning, informing him of her whereabouts.

Clover was a small town with limited choices in accommodations. She knew that several options, like the quaint B and B and a small hotel, would probably be closed by now. But the chain hotel still had its lights on and, as she got closer, the vacancy sign gave her hope. To her relief the young man at the receptionist desk didn't appear to know her and apparently hadn't been paying attention to the news. He didn't even question her saying that she'd gotten into town late and was temporarily without her car.

"Have a good evening," he said mechanically as he handed her a key.

"And I'm expecting no visitors," she informed him. "I do not want to be disturbed."

He nodded sleepily. "No problem. It's been pretty quiet here tonight."

She thanked him with a stiff smile then headed out to find her room, but as she went down the sidewalk she looked all around, trying to be sure that no one had followed her...no one was watching. The earlier numbness was fading.

But feeling somewhat assured that she was safe, she entered her room and locked the door, making sure that the sliding glass door that led to the courtyard was secure as well. Then, completely and utterly exhausted, she fell onto the bed fully dressed and cried herself to sleep.

When she awoke it was to the sound of the sliding glass door slowly opening. A flash of sunlight illuminated the otherwise dark room and she could hear the sound of someone pushing through the heavy drapes. Too afraid to lift her head and look, she simply remained frozen, afraid to breathe and wondering if she could grab her gun from the bedside table before this intruder could make it to her. She was about to make a fast leap for the gun when the sound of someone pounding on the door, stopped her cold. *There were two of them? Trapping her in this hotel room?*

SIXTEEN

"Who's there?" she yelled. And then she screamed out at the top of her lungs. "Help!"

"It's Logan!" he yelled loudly, still pounding on the door. *"Are you okay?"*

"Logan!" In one swift move, she leaped from the bed, grabbed the handgun and opened the door. Behind her she heard the slider door slam shut, but when she looked back, no one was there. "Oh, Logan!" She fell into his arms.

"What's going on?" he demanded with a frantic expression. "Why did you—"

"Someone was in here," she gasped, pointing to the slider door. "They'd just broken into my room and—"

He pushed her behind him, rushing over to the door to peer out, looking both ways and all around. "It looks like the door was jimmied. But I don't see anyone out there." He closed and locked it, pulling out his phone. "What happened?"

As she explained the moments before he got there, he put in a phone call to Stan Griggs, relaying the information to him. "I didn't even see the guy," she told him. "So I don't have any description. He ran out when you were banging on the door."

"That's right," Logan told Griggs. "No, I didn't see anything. It's room 107. First floor. Less than five minutes ago."

Then he thanked him and pocketed his phone. "He's sending someone here to investigate."

"I don't know what I'd have done if you hadn't banged on that door. I was so scared I could barely breathe. And my gun was just out of reach. I'm so glad you showed up just now!" Tears of gratitude and relief filled her eyes. *"Thank you!"*

He gathered her into his arms, holding her tight and stroking her hair. "I was so worried about you, Mallory. I didn't know where you were, or what had happened. Why did you take off like that?"

"I don't know. I was confused. Didn't know what to do." She clung to him, never wanting to let go.

"Why didn't you tell me you were going?"

"I figured you were asleep. And I meant to text you first thing this morning." She let out a ragged sigh. "I'm so sorry, Logan."

He pushed her hair away from her face, looking down with such an intensity that her feelings of pure terror slowly melted away. "I don't know what I'd do if anything happened to you. Please, Mallory, tell me why you left the firehouse?"

She felt more tears coming now. "It's hard to explain," she said as she reached for a tissue. "But Jennifer seemed upset about me being there last night."

"What?" He looked angry. "What did she do? What did she say?"

"You can't really blame her." Mallory sat down on the chair, pulling her knees up to her chin and wrapping her arms around them. "In her eyes, I look like a dangerous person. A murder suspect. Wherever I go, someone gets hurt. I'm sure she honestly believed she was in danger with me there."

"But that's ridiculous."

"No, not really." She shook her head. "All she had to go by was the news. You have to admit it makes me look bad."

He sighed as he sat down on the other chair. "I guess I understand that."

"And I was certain you'd be asleep." She waved to the rumpled queen-size bed. "And I have to admit that I just had the best night's sleep I've had in days. Well, except for my rude awakening." She glanced at the alarm clock, surprised to see it was past eight.

He exhaled loudly. "I just wish I'd known. You had me so worried."

"I'm really sorry. I never meant to worry you." She frowned. "How did you find me, anyway?"

"I drove around town, asking myself where I would go if I needed a bed in the middle of the night. This was the first place I looked."

"But I told the motel clerk not to let anyone know I was here."

"Fortunately Brian is a friend of mine. And it helps that I'm the fire chief." He grinned. "You hungry for breakfast?"

She pushed a strand of stray hair away from her face. "Kinda. But I'd like to clean up a little first."

"Do you want me to go wait in the lobby while you grab a shower?"

She glanced over at the recently jimmied door. "I'm not sure I feel safe."

"Do you want me to wait here?" He looked slightly uncomfortable, too. "Or, if you like, you can come back to the firehouse and use the facilities there. That's a safe place. And I'll let Jennifer know she needs to keep her opinions to herself."

She reluctantly agreed and before long, she had the women's shower room all to herself. But as much as she wanted to relax, she still felt shaken and frightened from the intruder this morning. If it was that easy to break into her locked hotel room, how much easier would it be for a killer to just walk into the firehouse, where no doors were even locked? How hard would it be for the killer to walk into this shower room? As Mallory hurried to shower and dry and dress, she wondered if she would ever escape these fears. Was anywhere safe?

SEVENTEEN

Logan suspected that, after last night's encounter, Mallory wouldn't care to eat at the firehouse this morning. And she probably wouldn't be all that comfortable in a restaurant, either. He considered taking her to his place, but after hearing about her hotel room intruder, it didn't seem prudent to have breakfast in a fishbowl.

So, while Mallory was in the shower, he decided to call his mother. Not only did she live in a safe and secluded neighborhood, she probably wouldn't mind letting him use her car. And driving around town in his highly visible red Jeep felt risky.

"You got anything good over there for breakfast?" he asked.

She laughed. "Well, I could. If I thought someone was coming. Selma spent the night at Naomi's last night so I was just sitting here with my coffee and the newspaper."

"Do you mind having company?"

"Since when are you considered company?" she teased.

"Actually, I'd like to bring someone with me, if you don't mind."

"Not at all. Who?"

"A woman friend," he said the words slowly, knowing that it was like waving a checkered flag in front of his mom.

"A woman friend?"

"It's Mallory Myers," he said quickly. "Maybe you've been reading about her in your newspaper. But just so you know, you can't believe everything you read."

There was a short silence and he wondered if he'd lost his connection. "I *have* been reading about her, Logan. Is she really with you?"

"I've been helping her, Mom. And, trust me, she's not who they're portraying her to be in the news. In fact, she's been in a lot of danger. And maybe it's not a good idea to bring her to—"

"You bring her right over here," his mom insisted. "If you believe in her, I do, too. And Selma's been saying the same thing. She thinks that the news has got it all wrong."

"We can't stay long," he warned her. "And I have an ulterior motive." Now he explained that his idea to switch cars with her. "If you don't mind, I'll leave my Jeep in the garage and take your Subaru. I think we'll be safer since half the folks in town seem to drive a Subaru."

"That's just fine. I don't plan on going anywhere today, anyway."

When Mallory returned from her shower, in an amazingly short time, he told her they had an invitation to breakfast.

"You're not going to tell me where we're going?" she asked as he drove a circuitous route through town.

"Not yet." He made another left turn. "Keep an eye on that gray pickup," he told her as he continued in the opposite direction of his mom's gated neighborhood. "See if you can read the plate. I think we're being followed." But after several more turns, the pickup disappeared and, with no other cars in sight, he made a beeline to his mom's development, punching the security code into the gated entrance and quickly getting in.

With no one following him, he drove directly to his

mom's house, where she'd already parked her Subaru in the driveway, leaving the garage open for his Jeep.

"You're certainly making yourself at home," Mallory observed as they got out of the Jeep inside the garage. He grinned as he pushed the switch on the wall to close the door.

"It used to be home," he said as he opened the back door and yelled, "Hello."

He quickly introduced Mallory to his mom and, just as he expected, there was a nice little breakfast all ready for them. The three of them visited as they ate, and he was encouraged by how well Mallory and his mom seemed to hit it off. But when they finished he was antsy. Even though he knew no one followed him here, the idea of endangering his mother and sister was more than he could handle.

"Hate to eat and run, but I'd like to get over to the hospital," he told his mom. "Check on things."

"Thank you for the lovely breakfast," Mallory said. "Best one I've had in days."

His mom hugged them both, warned them to be careful, and after he checked out the window to be sure no one suspicious was lurking about, he hurried Mallory out to the Subaru and they headed for the hospital.

As he drove, Mallory seemed to relax, raving about how sweet his mother was. "Yeah," he agreed. "She's all right."

"Do you think Winnie's still in the hospital?" Mallory asked as they hurried across the parking lot.

"For a sprained ankle? I doubt it." He glanced cautiously around as they walked through the lobby. Hopefully it wasn't risky to come here like this. But he felt fairly certain that the security was high. From what he'd heard, Antonio Perez was being closely guarded. And judging by the cruisers in the parking lot, it appeared that even the state police had been called in. He stopped at the information desk to make an inquiry about Winnie—their pretense for coming here—but was surprised to learn she hadn't been released yet.

When they found her in her room, she explained that her foot injury was worse than they'd thought. "It was broken in two places. They did surgery and put some pins in," she told them. "But I get to go home this afternoon."

"That's good." Logan smiled.

"Did you hear about Perez?" Winnie asked.

"What do you mean?"

"He died."

"What?" Mallory's eyes grew wide.

"When?" Logan demanded.

"Around five this morning." Winnie nodded. "Yep. That's the scuttlebutt."

"But I thought he was only listed in serious condition," Mallory said.

"That's what Griggs told me last night," Logan said. "What happened?"

"I don't know," Winnie said. "I guess it was worse than they thought."

"That's too bad…" Logan knew it was senseless to feel guilty…but he did.

"It's not your fault," Winnie told him. "You did what you had to do."

"That's right," Mallory agreed. "Don't blame yourself."

"If you ask me, he got just what he deserved," Winnie declared. "Think about it, Logan, if you hadn't stopped him last night, he might've killed all of us."

"Maybe…" Logan checked his watch.

"I wonder if the police got a chance to question him before he died," Mallory said quietly.

"Trent was here last night," Winnie told them. "He might know something."

"Was he surprised about Perez?" Logan asked her. "I

mean, since he'd been so certain that Mallory wasn't in any kind of danger yesterday."

"He was surprised that I got hurt running from Perez." Winnie chuckled. "I told him I could've been shot. And it would've been his fault, since I'd come out there to bring him that pizza."

"What'd he say about that?" Logan said absently.

"He wanted to know what happened to the pizza."

"That sounds about right," Mallory told her.

"Well, I'm glad to see you're okay," Logan told Winnie. "I'm guessing you won't be ready to return to work for a while."

"I've got to do some physical therapy," she told them. "Not sure how long that will—" She stopped talking and waved toward the door. "Hey, Trent, good buddy," she called out. "What's up?"

Dressed in his deputy uniform, Trent entered the room with a serious expression. "Just checking to see how you're doing," he told Winnie. "Hello, Logan, Miss Myers. Sounds like you all had a pretty exciting time after I left last night. Sorry to miss out."

"Why did you leave?" Logan asked Trent.

He shrugged. "Seemed pretty quiet to me. And there was a call about kids drag-racing over on Northridge Road. Thought I should go check it out."

"Everyone okay?"

"Yeah. They were gone by the time I got there."

"So, what are you doing here?" Logan asked.

"Working on the Perez investigation." Trent pointed at Mallory. "I know Deputy Griggs questioned you last night, but I'd like to ask you a few more questions." He looked at Logan. "You, too."

"How about me?" Winnie asked in a little-girl voice.

"We already got your story last night," Trent told her.

"Maybe we should go somewhere else," Logan suggested to Trent. "Let Winnie get some rest."

When they got settled in a small office that law enforcement was allowed to use, Logan studied Trent closely. What he wanted to know, but was hesitant to ask, was why was Trent doing this investigation. Instead, he hoped to appear cooperative and perhaps extract some information from Trent. "I was sorry to hear that Perez died," Logan told him. "The last I heard it sounded like he was going to make it."

Trent just nodded. "We were surprised by that, too." He turned to Mallory. "Which brings me to the first question I have for you."

"Yeah?"

"Where were you last night?"

"When?"

"From the time you left your house." He glanced at his notes. "That was about ten-thirty."

Mallory glanced nervously at Logan.

"I took her to the firehouse with me," he said. "We felt she'd be safer there."

"Yes. I was aware of that. But where did you spend the night, Mallory?" He narrowed his eyes. "I know for a fact you were not at the firehouse."

"That's true. I could tell that I was making one of the crew members nervous," she explained. "So I walked over to the hotel. I stayed there."

"By yourself?"

"Yes," she answered in an irritated tone. "By myself."

"And did you leave the hotel at any time during the night or early morning?"

"No, I was there the whole time. Asleep." She frowned at him.

"And your car was at your parents' house."

"Yes. Unless it took itself for a spin without me."

Trent glared at her. "Just answer the questions, please."

"Why are you interrogating me like this?"

Ignoring her, Trent pointed to Logan. "And you spent the night at the firehouse, right? That's what I was told."

"Yes. I was there all night."

"You never left in the early hours of the morning?"

"No. I just said I was there all night. I didn't leave until around eight this morning."

"And where did you go?"

"Looking for Mallory."

"So you weren't aware that she was staying at the hotel?"

"No. I thought she was in the women's quarters." Logan glanced at Mallory.

"And you believe her? That she went to the hotel and never left there?"

"Of course." Logan frowned. "Why are you asking us this stuff, Trent? You're obviously working on some half-cooked theory here. How about sharing it with us?"

"We have reason to believe that Antonio Perez didn't die from the gunshot wound."

Logan felt slightly relieved, but also curious. "How did he die?"

"We think it was suffocation." Trent kept his eyes on Mallory. "The coroner will make a determination, but it appears that a pillow was held over his head. Because of his connection to the Portland crime, the state police are conducting an investigation right now."

"But the way you've been questioning us? Do you think we're suspects?" Logan asked.

"Not particularly you. It will be easy to establish you spent the night at the firehouse."

"So are you suggesting that Mallory is a suspect? Because if she is, you probably should've read her her rights."

"This isn't an official investigation." Trent gave them a creepy smile. "Just friends talking to friends." He turned to Logan now. "By the way, I didn't see your vehicle out there. What are you driving?"

"If this isn't an official investigation, I probably don't have to tell you." Logan reached for Mallory's hand. "We should go."

"But why are you focusing on me?" Mallory asked Trent. "I was devastated to learn that Perez died. I wanted him to expose Brock for being behind all of this."

"Oh, I'm sure you did." Trent gave a knowing nod.

"I don't know how you can possibly solve this thing if you've made up your mind that Mallory is guilty," Logan said as he led Mallory to the door.

"Yeah." Mallory shook her finger at him. "Why are you wasting time with me when you could be going after the real criminals?"

"And what about surveillance cameras?" Logan asked before they went out. "The hospital is probably loaded with them. Why aren't you looking at that footage?"

"Be assured, we are. But the camera that would've picked up the perpetrator going into Perez's room just happened to be covered." Trent glared at Mallory. "With a woman's T-shirt. Does that ring a bell with anyone?"

Logan felt Mallory's hand tightening around his. "Let's go," he told her.

"Better watch your back, Logan." Trent followed them to the door. "You might be hanging with a very dangerous woman."

Mallory stopped to lock eyes with Trent. "If I'm that dangerous, why not just arrest me right now?"

Trent's smile was dipped in smugness. "Don't worry. It's just a matter of time."

"Come on," Logan urged Mallory. "Let's get out of here." He tugged her out the door and down the hall toward the elevator. "Trent is certifiably nuts," he said once they were alone in the elevator. "What makes him think you killed Perez?"

Mallory didn't answer.

Logan punched the lobby button. "Seriously, why is he so focused on you? Why isn't he out looking for the real killer? What motive could you possibly have for killing Perez?"

Mallory looked into his eyes. "Maybe they think I hired Perez," she said quietly.

"But why?"

"To make it look like I was in danger."

Logan stared at her. "That's crazy."

"Everything about this is crazy," she whispered as the doors opened. "It is my never-ending nightmare."

Still holding her hand, Logan guided her through the lobby. But his mind was occupied, trying to put together some kind of plan. He needed a way to keep her safe. Away from whatever force seemed intent on destroying her.

And, yes, a tiny part of him was suddenly questioning his involvement with her. What if Trent was right? What if Logan was completely wrong about her? What if she truly was a criminal? As they went outside, he glanced at her and, seeing a silent tear streaking down her flushed cheek, he felt certain he wasn't wrong. But he knew that even if he was wrong, it was too late to turn back. His heart was already in—over-his-head in.

He paused under a tree. "We're going to get through this," he told her gently. "We're going to prove your innocence."

She looked hopefully up at him. "You believe in me?"

He leaned down close to her, soaking in her sweet smell, getting lost in her big brown eyes. "It's more than just believing in you," he assured her. And then he kissed her, holding her close for a few seconds. "Much more," he said quietly.

EIGHTEEN

"I want to talk to Stan Griggs," Mallory told Logan as he drove through the hospital parking lot. "I want to hear his take on what happened with Perez."

"Good idea." Logan nodded. "Why don't you give him a call?"

Mallory pulled out her phone. "And I want to go home and do some more research on my dad's computer today. I want to start putting together a news story."

"A news story?"

"Yeah. An exposé on Brock and everything that's gone down these past few days. If I can't get Alex to push it at *Channel Six*, I'll send it to another station." She hit the speed dial for Griggs.

"You sure that's a good idea?" Logan sounded concerned. "What if Brock decides to sue you for libel?"

"Telling the truth is not libel. And I intend on getting the truth." She heard Griggs say "Hello" and quickly explained her need to talk to him. "If you're not too busy."

"It's my day off, but I'd like to talk to you, Mallory. Come on by the house. I'm just raking pine needles." She thanked him and hung up, taking a moment to check for messages. "I haven't gotten any anonymous texts today," she said as she dropped her phone in her bag. "I wonder what that means."

"You don't think they came from Perez?"

She considered this. "I wondered if some of them did. But then I got that last one after Perez was shot."

"If they did come from Perez, the police should get to the bottom of it when they look into his phone."

"Originally, I had assumed they were all from Brock but it makes sense that he'd want his hit man to do his dirty phone work. Harder to trace back to him."

Logan was taking another circuitous route, but she suspected he was headed for his mom's house. "You going to switch cars?" she asked.

"Yeah. Now that we're done here in town."

"Yeah, probably best to keep her out of this." Mallory pursed her lips, trying to think of the right way to say what she knew needed to be said. "And after you drop me at my parents' place...well, I'd like you to keep out of it too, Logan."

"Huh?" He turned to look at her.

"I just don't think you should be around me. Trent was right about something."

"What?"

"I am dangerous."

"What on earth are you saying?"

"It's dangerous to be associated with me, Logan. It's a risk I can't ask you to take."

"You don't have to ask me. I'm already here, Mallory. I'm fully on board."

"But after seeing your mom this morning. And thinking about Selma. And how much they need and depend on you. Well, I have to ask you to step aside. Besides, my dad should be here soon." She checked her phone again for an update.

"Soon? The last text I got from him, he was hung up in Chicago with a standby ticket to Denver."

"His last-minute trip has been a mess, but he'll probably be here this afternoon."

"Until then?"

"Until then, I'm asking you to step aside, Logan."

"You can *ask* me to step aside, but that doesn't mean I will."

She clenched her fists. "You *have* to, Logan."

He didn't respond as he pulled into his mom's driveway, using the remote on the visor to open the garage door. Once they were inside, he told her he'd be right back. While he went into the house, she got into the Jeep. She was resolved. Whether he liked it or not, she was going to cut him loose. As soon as he dropped her at home, she would put her foot down and insist that he leave. She realized now how selfish she'd been by allowing him to help her. His only hope for safety would be to get away from her. Far, far away.

They were both silent as he drove out of town. Mallory pretended to be focused on her phone, but her mind was engaged in a battle. Part of her knew what had to be done—she needed to firmly tell Logan to get lost. The other part of her wanted to cling to him for dear life. She wasn't even sure which side would win.

"Here we are," he said as he pulled into her parents' driveway.

"Thank you for everything," she said in a businesslike tone. "I really appreciate it. But I can handle it on my own from here on out."

"Really?" He turned to stare at her. "You honestly think you don't need my help. What about this morning? You thought you'd be safe in the hotel, but how did that work out for you?"

She pressed her lips together. Of course, she needed his help. That wasn't the point. "I appreciate your help. But I have a plan now," she told him. "A plan that does not include you."

Logan frowned.

"I'm going to see Deputy Griggs." She opened the door. "If necessary, I'll take refuge at their house. Thank you for all your help, Logan. But this is where we part ways. Okay?" She hurried to get out of the car, heading for the house. But by the time she reached the front door, he was right behind her.

"No," he was saying, "that's not okay."

She turned to look at him, seeing the hurt in his eyes. "I'm sorry," she said quietly. "But I have to stick to my guns on this."

"Look." He grabbed her hand. "I get that you need to be safe. And maybe staying at the Griggs's is a good plan. But cutting me loose, like you're doing, isn't." He peered into her eyes. "I haven't been sticking around just to be gallant, Mallory. I really do care about you."

She felt her resolve dwindling. "I really care about you, too, Logan. But Trent is right—they all are—I *am* dangerous. Until I can expose Brock and somehow prove he's been behind all of this, I will continue to be dangerous. Can't you see that?"

He barely nodded. "Let's make a deal, okay?"

"What kind of deal?"

"Let me go with you to talk to Deputy Griggs. If I'm convinced you'll be safe at their house, I'll back off. Okay?"

She considered this.

"I've got to keep my word to your dad, Mallory. I promised him I'd keep you safe. I can't just abandon you now."

"Okay," she agreed. "You can follow me over to the Griggs place."

As Mallory drove the couple of miles to the Griggs's place, a property on ten acres and not too different from her parents', she tried to remember the last time she'd been at their house. It'd probably been close to ten years, an anniversary party that she'd attended with her parents when she was a teen. But she knew that Gloria and Stan were completely trustworthy. They'd been good friends and neighbors of her parents for as long as she could remember. As she pulled into their driveway, she spotted Stan out in front. Dressed in shorts and a Hawaiian shirt, he was casually raking pine needles. But he set his rake aside and waved, greeting them both as they got out of their separate vehicles.

"Come on inside," he told them. "I'm ready for a break." He wiped his damp brow with the back of his hand as he opened the front. "Already getting hot out here." He led them into the great room. "Sorry about the mess. I've been baching it the last few days. Gloria took Lucy to visit her mother and won't be back until next week." He moved some clutter off the couch, making room.

Logan tossed Mallory a questioning glance, but she ignored it. "Thanks for letting me come talk to you." She sat down.

"Well, I've been wanting to talk to you, too. So this is handy."

"Trent told us that Perez may have been murdered last night," she began.

"His death looked pretty suspicious, and it's under investigation." Stan seemed to be studying her. "Did Deputy Fallows question you about it?"

She nodded. "He acted like I was a suspect." She looked him directly in the eyes. "Is that true?"

"Well, everyone with any connection to Perez would be a suspect." He pointed to Logan. "Including you."

"I gathered that." Logan leaned back, crossing his arms in front of him.

"But neither of us had anything to do with it," Mallory told Stan.

"Well, actually, I did," Logan admitted. "I mean, I did shoot the man last night."

"Yes, but he didn't die from a gunshot wound," Mallory pointed out. "And that was self-defense."

"My question is, why would someone be motivated to slip into the hospital and finish Perez off?" Stan asked.

"My question is, where was security when this happened?" Logan leaned forward. "I thought Perez was going to be under close surveillance last night. Seems to me that someone fell asleep on the job."

Stan nodded. "Yeah, I had the same thought. But according to Deputy Zimmerman, Perez was so out of it that they didn't have any concern about flight risk. As a result, the security probably wasn't as tight as it should've been. To be fair, no one suspected that Perez's life was in danger. We were all caught off guard."

"You asked who would be motivated to kill Perez?" Mallory persisted. "I can tell you who."

Stan's bushy brows arched. "Yes?"

And so she began to pour out all the details of her story about Brock and Kestra and her theory that Perez was working for Brock. "I know it's a lot to take in," she said finally, "but if I could just get law enforcement to listen to me. To take me seriously. Someone besides my dad, that is. And he should be here by tomorrow morning."

Stan rubbed his chin. "Wow, Mallory. That's quite a story."

"I know it sounds crazy," she admitted. "But I've been researching Brock. He has a past history that he doesn't want anyone to know about. When he thought I was going to expose him he went ballistic. The man comes across as Prince Charming on the air, but in real life he's a narcissist and a bully. And I feel certain that he hired Perez to kill me. And I'm equally certain that Perez is the one who murdered Kestra." She frowned. "The part of this I can't explain yet is who killed Perez. But I'm guessing that whoever did it is connected to Brock."

"And the guy who drove us off the road," Logan added, "he's got to be mixed up in this, too. Has anyone been able to get him to talk?"

"Not that I've heard," Stan told him. "But if what you're saying is true—"

"It is true!" she insisted.

"In your mind, but it hasn't been proven yet," Stan pointed out. "But if you're right. If Dennison is behind this whole thing, it stands to reason that he wouldn't want Perez to talk. Whoever killed him may have been paid to shut Perez up."

"Yes." Mallory nodded eagerly. "That must be it."

"So that means we still have a murderer around," Logan added. "And Mallory is still in danger."

Stan's brow creased. "I think you're right. I'm going to text Sheriff Lambert, suggesting he put a guard on Sean Forney."

They waited for him to finish with his phone, then Logan spoke up. "Mallory was hoping she could spend the night at your place," he said. "I told her that I wasn't going to leave her side unless I knew she was safe. Just like I promised Deputy Myers."

"When's he getting home, anyway?"

"Good question." Mallory quickly explained the red-eye and standby flights.

"Might've been quicker to just drive." Stan frowned. "Well, you're welcome to stay here if you want, Mallory. But I'm working the night shift tonight so you'd be on your own."

Logan gave her a concerned look.

"Oh." She bit her lip.

"So maybe you don't want to be too quick to get rid of me," Logan said in a teasing tone.

"You better hang on to this guy," Stan told her. "And you kids can stay here if you want, but it's pretty isolated, too."

"Where do you think the safest place for her to stay would be?" Logan asked eagerly. "I thought the firehouse was a good solution, but she ended up spending the night at the hotel when one of my firefighters insulted her."

"I'm not sure that being in town is going to be any safer than her folks' house." Stan got a thoughtful look.

"Maybe you could just lock me up in jail," Mallory suggested.

Stan laughed. "That seems a bit extreme."

"But at least everyone would be safe," she argued.

"What makes you think a jail is any safer than a hospital?" Logan asked her.

"Oh…good point." She frowned.

"I've got an idea," Stan said suddenly. "You go ahead and stay at your folks' house again tonight. Park your car right out front like before. Make it look like you're there by yourself. But we'll be camped out all around the place. We'll set up a trap."

"But won't that be dangerous?" Logan asked. "I mean, for Mallory."

"We'll be armed and ready, and if anyone tries to get into the house, we'll get to him first."

"Yes," Mallory told him. "That might work."

"If we do it right, it will work," Stan assured her.

"What if no one shows?" she asked Stan. "And your stakeout is for nothing?"

"Better than the other way around." Stan turned to Logan. "Do you mind staying with her tonight? I want her to appear to be alone, but I really don't think she should be on her own. I know her daddy would agree with me on that."

"No problem. I already told her I'm sticking around until this whole thing is wrapped up. Believe me, I'm not backing down."

"You can leave your Jeep here," Stan told him. "And

keep a low profile over there. Maybe sneak into the house. Probably the sooner the better. And you kids stay in Jim's office like you did before. It's a good safe room. And don't be worried. We'll have deputies staked out all around. If a perpetrator shows up, we'll nab him."

"And this time you'll keep him alive?" Mallory asked hopefully. "So he can talk?"

"That's the plan. But don't give up on Sean Forney. He still might talk." Stan slowly stood, walking them to the front door. "Mostly I just want you to be careful, Mallory. Both of you." He shook Logan's hand. "And I'm sure Mallory's dad will be relieved to know you're still watching over his little girl."

"I just don't want to be the cause of anyone else getting hurt," she said quietly.

"You're not the cause," Logan told her as they went outside.

She didn't argue with him, but she knew better. If she had never been associated with Brock Dennison, if she had never dated him, never discovered his dark history… none of them would be in danger. But also, she reminded herself, she wouldn't be spending all this time with Logan. That was worth something. As long as he didn't get hurt. If Logan got hurt, she would never forgive herself.

NINETEEN

Logan got a phone call from Griggs shortly after lunch. "I just wanted you to know the findings on the break-in while Mallory was at the hotel. I just learned that it's happened several times this summer. The sliding doors have been jimmied in the same manner. The intruder slips in, steals the guests' purses or wallets while they're sleeping then takes off. No one gets hurt."

"So, that's all it was."

"Seems like it. Although I can't give you any guarantees."

"So we can breathe a little more easily?"

"I'm not saying that, either. Like I told you, we didn't find signs of anyone else out there last night. And, as you know, we've had deputies scouting around there all day. We're combing that whole section of the National Forest. So far, we haven't found another vehicle. And the guy in lockdown, Sean Forney, isn't talking, but I suspect he's in cahoots with Perez. My thinking is that he dropped off Perez shortly after they ran you off the road yesterday. I'm guessing they set up some kind of hideout in the woods. We put a request to get some canine units in there to sniff around. But sounds like they won't be available until tomorrow afternoon."

"That's interesting to know," Logan told him. "But until

this thing is completely wrapped up, until we know who killed Perez, I don't think we should let our guard down."

"No, of course, not," Griggs said firmly. "To be honest, I'm not sure it's wise for you two to stay out there. I wish her old man was back."

"Me, too. He's still stuck in Chicago, but he thinks he has a seat on a late flight tonight. Hopefully he'll be here by early morning."

"Well, I'm glad you're sticking by her, Logan. I'd hate to think of her being out there by herself."

After they finished the call, Logan decided to take a nap. He suggested that Mallory do the same, just in case they had another long night ahead. But she seemed wide awake and energized, eager to do some work on her dad's computer. As he felt himself dozing off in a guest room, he imagined her immersed in her research, pecking away on the keyboard, hopefully making some brilliant discoveries.

After a nice long nap, he woke up feeling surprisingly refreshed. Being holed up in the Myers's house—in the middle of a hot summer's day with the AC running—wasn't half-bad. And, knowing the place was crawling with law enforcement and more on the way this evening, he felt relatively assured that they were out of harm's way.

Logan tapped quietly on the bear cave door. "I don't know the secret password," he said as she opened it. "But I am glad you kept it locked."

"And I'm glad you're awake." Mallory waved him in. "Wait until you hear what I've uncovered."

"Fire away." He opened the cooler and removed a soda, taking it with him to the sofa where he made himself comfortable.

"For starters, I got an email back from the news station that Brock worked for down in LA." Her eyes were bright with enthusiasm. "A female member of their staff made a sexual harassment complaint against Brock. No charges were filed, but he was fired and never contested it."

"Uh-huh."

"But that's not all. I discovered where Brock went to high school. It's this rural town in Wisconsin. I had no idea he'd ever lived there. But there was a lot he didn't tell me. Anyway, I located a couple of his old high school classmates with social media. A woman named Anna remembered him well and was willing to talk.

"Turns out that Brock had a reputation with the ladies even back then—a reputation for being abusive. Anna told me about a good friend of hers named Jeanette who should've filed criminal charges against Brock, but she was too embarrassed to go public. And Anna suspected that Jeanette wasn't the only one. She still lives in the same town and even offered to do some more investigating for me."

"This is important information," Logan told her. "But it still doesn't prove that Brock's guilty of murder—or more specifically of hiring someone to kill you."

"Maybe not, but it makes a good story." She pointed to the computer screen. "I've been putting it all together. Almost done."

"You plan to hand this off to your news writer friend in Portland?"

"I already sent Alex an email, sharing a few interesting tidbits—like how Brock's college girlfriend mysteriously disappeared. And I told him there's more coming." She frowned. "But I haven't heard back from him. Maybe I should give him a call just to make sure he got it."

"And you're sure you can't be sued for libel or slander?"

"I'm only giving Alex the facts. I'm citing resources and dates and information that are available to the public. Just like a normal news story. And I'm sending the same document to Detective Janice Doyle, too. If they don't start sniffing around Brock by Monday—well, I might just call the FBI. For all we know, they might already have Brock on one of their wanted lists." Now she spun the chair back around and continued to type.

"You are a force to be reckoned with."

"Kestra's memorial service is probably just finishing up by now."

"Wish you were there?"

"Not really. Not after I heard Brock was giving her eulogy. That is just so wrong."

"It is pretty creepy."

"But I do feel like I should've been there…she was my best friend…except that no one would've wanted me there."

"Well, you can be with Kestra in your heart," he said quietly. "That's what really matters, huh?"

She nodded.

"I'm going to go peek around," he told her. "I want to see if I can spot any of the deputies lurking about."

"Are you going outside?" she asked with a look of alarm.

"Nah. I'll just peek out the windows. We're under Deputy Griggs's orders now. To stay inside and out of sight."

"And he said to avoid the windows," she reminded him. "Be careful."

"That's my middle name."

As he walked through the house, he wondered about Deputy Griggs's plan. It had seemed to make sense earlier, but now he wasn't so sure. Three deputies didn't seem like a lot. He peeked through the crack in the drapes over the front window. It looked perfectly deserted out there. Just lots of trees and sunshine. And there, out in front of the garage, Mallory's car was parked. Like a sitting duck.

Staying down low, just in case someone was out there watching the house—someone besides the deputies—he slipped into the kitchen, got a couple of apples from the fridge and headed back to the bear cave.

"Want one?" he asked Mallory as he relocked the dead bolt on the door.

"No, thanks." Her previous cheerful demeanor appeared to have vanished.

"Something wrong?"

She frowned. "Maybe."

"What's up?" he asked as he sat down.

"Alex is gone."

"Gone? You mean, like he has the day off?"

"No. According to the newsroom receptionist, Alex got fired."

"Fired?"

She nodded.

"When did that happen? Was it because of the story the other newscaster read last night?"

"I have no idea. It was like pulling teeth just to get Gina to admit that he'd been fired. And I used to think she was a friend of mine, too. But I have a feeling my name is mud there now. Thanks to Brock."

"Did you try to call Alex?"

"I only have his work number. Of course, that doesn't work."

"What about the story you were sending him? Do you think he got that?"

"That's what's really worrying me." She grimaced. "If Alex got fired, someone else would have access to his computer...his email...who knows who might've read it? And because it's from me...well, I'm pretty sure that I've lost my job, too." Her chin quivered slightly. "And I know that seems small in light of everything else. But it's all so unfair. It's like no matter what I do or how hard I try to figure it all out, this thing doesn't go away. It doesn't become more manageable. It only gets worse." She started to cry. "It feels so hopeless."

He went over and wrapped his arms around her. "I know

it sounds like a cliché, Mallory, but things really do look the darkest before the dawn. And just because Alex is gone doesn't mean that you can't share your story with someone else. What about your idea to send it to another news station? Imagine if another station broke your story for you. Wouldn't that be cool? I mean it's a pretty big story. I'd think any station would be thrilled to get their hands on it."

She sniffed. "It is a big story."

"So why not share it with the competition?"

"Okay." She nodded. "I will."

"Do news stations watch their competition's news shows?" He took a bite of the apple.

"They sure do!" She turned back to the keyboard. "And Brock will be fit to be tied when he hears *Channel Two News* telling his story."

Logan heard his phone ringing and when he checked the caller ID he saw it was Deputy Griggs. "Hey, Griggs," he said. "What's up?"

"Good news!"

"What's that?"

"We caught Perez's other accomplice."

"*Really?* You're certain?"

"Yep. His name is Damien Sanders. And there was a second vehicle. Another SUV, registered to Sean Forney, the guy in jail. This proves these three thugs were linked. Sanders, Perez and Forney. Forney's rig was parked off Harner Road, pretty deep in the woods. Amazing that he was even spotted."

"Harner Road's not too far from here."

"That's right. Anyway, this SUV is just loaded with evidence, too. Maps of the forest. GPS to the Myerses' house. Might take us a few days to work our way through everything. But we got him locked up on probation violations. And it looks like Sean Forney has links to the mob. Probably why he's keeping his mouth shut. We found illegal firearms as well as a small packet of cocaine. We'll set the bail pretty high."

"Good to know." Logan tapped Mallory on the shoulder. *"They got the third guy,"* he whispered.

"And one of the deputies said that he's pretty sure that same SUV was at the hotel—about the same time as the break-in to Mallory's room."

"So it wasn't just a burglar."

"Maybe not. We'll figure that one out later. But I thought you'd want to know."

"This is good news, Stan."

"We even spotted some arson stuff in the SUV. Some kind of incendiary device. It was like hitting the jackpot."

"That's great!" Logan gave Mallory a big smile.

"So, you kids don't need to be too concerned now."

"Right…"

"I'm not saying you should let your guard down completely, Logan. But we feel pretty certain we got our man. And as far as we can tell, it was just the three of them. Perez and Sanders and Forney. We've been calling them the Three Stooges. There's no sign of anyone else involved. And Sanders is on his way to join Forney in the county jail right now. Forney's not talking, but that's probably due to his mob connections. We're hoping we can work the two of them against each other. Hopefully we'll get a confession out of one of them before the night is over. And thanks to Sanders's parole violations he'll be in lockdown for a long time."

"That's great."

"Well, I just thought you'd want to know. And pick up your Jeep anytime you like."

"I will. Thanks! Mallory is going to be hugely relieved."

"Hey, you guys should let her dad know, too. Maybe Jim can cancel that red-eye flight out of Chicago and head back to Iowa, save a few bucks, and enjoy the rest of his vacation now."

"Good idea." Logan told Griggs goodbye, then replayed the whole story to Mallory.

"That's fabulous!" First she did a happy dance and then she hugged Logan. "If this Sanders guy confesses, and exposes Brock, I'll be cleared!"

"And your troubles will be over." He held her close, breathing in the scent of her hair.

She let out a big sigh as she stepped away. "It's almost too good to believe. But what if they mess up somehow, what if this Sanders guy slips between their fingers? Or Brock works his magic and gets him set free? Or sends someone else to finish the job?"

Despite all Logan knew about Brock Dennison, and how much he trusted Mallory, there was still a tiny part of him that found it difficult to believe the smooth news anchor was truly behind all the madness of these past few days. Of course, he would never admit this much to Mallory. And he really hoped that it wouldn't be too long until her theory was proved right. "I don't think you need to worry about Sanders walking. It sounds like they've got him on enough parole violations to keep him locked up for quite a while. And I'm guessing they'll offer him a deal if he squeals on Dennison."

Her smile returned. "I'm sure you're right. It's just that I'm almost afraid to hope."

"Well, let it sink in. And Griggs suggested you call your dad right away. Maybe he won't need to end his vacation so abruptly now."

"Good thinking." She nodded eagerly as she reached for her phone. "The last time I talked to him was to tell him about the stakeout. But he'll be so relieved to hear the latest news. We can finally breathe easily."

Logan almost pointed out that Griggs had advised them

not to let their guard down completely just yet. But she was so happy, he hated to spoil it. Besides she was already talking to her dad. It would be good for her to relax a bit. He went over to look out the high window. Not to look for hidden assailants or law enforcement, but simply to enjoy the dappled afternoon sunlight filtering through the pines. He took in a deep breath. Mallory was right, it was time to breathe easily.

Even so, he would keep his guard up. At least until they got a full confession out of Sanders. And he did agree with Griggs, it seemed highly unlikely that there would be more than three bad guys on their tail. And even if there was a fourth, which just made no sense, it seemed even more unlikely that he'd stick around. With no vehicle to get away or hide out in. No accomplices to back him up. Possibly no weapons. Not to mention that their mission appeared hopelessly botched. If there was a fourth man, he would probably be long gone by now.

Logan turned to look at Mallory as she talked with her dad. He'd always thought she was very pretty, but with her big brown eyes bright with happiness and her voice so full of hope, she looked more beautiful than ever. It took all his self-control not to go over there and gather her up in his arms. But he wanted to pace himself.

He was no fool. He knew that part of what he had assumed was romance might simply be Mallory's need for protection. He'd shown up when she was at her most vulnerable. And what about when she tried to send him packing a few hours ago? If Griggs hadn't asked Logan to remain by her side, he'd probably be history by now. How would she view him when she realized she was truly safe? But, more than that, he knew there was a bigger threat to their relationship. What would happen when Mallory headed back to her apartment and job in the city?

Mallory told her dad goodbye, then turned to beam at

Logan. "I guess you were right." She set her phone down. "It really is darkest before the dawn."

"How about if we celebrate?" he said quickly, pushing his doubts about their relationship behind him. "Let me take you to dinner."

"That sounds great." But suddenly her smile faded. "Or not."

"What's wrong?" He frowned. Was it already happening? She was going to push him away? "Why not?"

"Well…it's just that half the people in town are already looking at me like I'm a murderer. That hasn't changed. And until this whole thing is totally cleared up—in *everyone's* eyes—it won't be much fun being out in the public eye."

"Oh…yeah, I guess I get that."

"So, how about I fix us dinner here again?" she offered.

"Sounds good." He felt his hopes lifting.

"And this time there won't be a big dark cloud hanging over our heads." Her face lit up. "And we can even use the barbecue grill without being afraid."

"And you might not know this, but I have a pretty hot reputation on the grill."

"Well, I figured you would. I mean, you are a fireman." She laughed.

"Is there anything you need?" he asked. "I could go town." Even as he offered this, he had reservations. He still wasn't quite ready to leave her on her own.

"I think we've got it covered from yesterday's grocery run." She opened the bear cave door. "No more being stuck in this stuffy room." She let out a happy whoop as she led the way down the hall. "And we can open the drapes and let some light in here."

"Sure. Why not?" Logan would still keep a watchful eye on things, but really it seemed as if the real danger was gone. Mostly he wanted to focus on Mallory tonight. He wanted to determine if what he'd been feeling was just his imagination, based on Mallory's desperate need for help, or something more. He hoped it was something more, but if he'd been deluded and Mallory politely thanked him for his help and sent him on his way, he would take it like a man. Still, it would hurt. More than he cared to think about, more than he'd ever admit.

TWENTY

Mallory tried not to be too disappointed that *Channel Two News* didn't run her story on their five o'clock news. But, she told herself, they probably didn't get it in time to check the facts. And it wouldn't be prudent to run a sensational story like that without proof. She wondered if they'd run it at ten.

"Want to watch the *Channel Six News*?" Logan asked.

"No, thanks." She firmly shook her head. "Mostly I'd like to forget about all of this…for a while, anyway."

"Works for me."

"Go ahead and finish watching that ballgame," she suggested as she put the fruit and green salads into the fridge. Everything for dinner was pretty much ready to go. But looking down at her shorts and the T-shirt that had a salad-dressing stain down the front, she decided to go clean up some. And feeling happy and celebratory, she longed to put on something more feminine for the evening. Unfortunately her clothing selection was pretty limited.

As Mallory was attempting to spruce up in the master bathroom, she suddenly remembered a couple of garments deep in the back of her mom's closet. "From my skinny days," her mom had said when Mallory was a young teen getting interested in fashion. But when her mom showed her the items, Mallory had made fun of them, saying how out of style they were. She wondered if she'd be so picky now. And, unless her memory had failed her, there was a bright floral sundress that could be fun.

So with Logan occupied by the baseball game, she snuck into her mom's walk-in closet. Hopefully Mom hadn't tossed her old clothes. Digging deep, Mallory discovered Mom's old wedding gown and an interesting tweed suit and there, hanging on a padded satin hanger, was the bright-colored sundress, looking surprisingly fresh and clean—as if it had rarely been worn.

She changed into the dress, and to her delight the bodice fit rather nicely. She went to the full-length mirror and realized it was actually a very pretty dress. She knew her mom would be thrilled to know Mallory liked it and wanted to wear it. So much so that Mallory ran to get her phone and, taking a quick selfie, sent it to her parents' phone. She could just imagine her mom showing it around to the aunts and cousins.

Then, since it was still pretty warm outside, she pinned her hair up in a messy bun and even borrowed a pair of her mom's earrings. Just simple gold hoops, but they felt fun and seemed to go with the vintage dress. Her mom would be pleased!

"Wow," Logan said when he spotted her walking into the kitchen. "I didn't know this was a formal dinner." He strolled in, carefully looking her over. "You look beautiful."

She felt her cheeks get warm. "It was my mom's dress—back in her premarriage, prechildren days. Before she put on the weight." She gave a little twirl, making the full skirt flow out. "But it's kinda fun."

"And it's stunning on you." Logan waved down to his dark blue fireman's T-shirt and khaki shorts. "I feel decidedly underdressed."

"You're just fine," she assured him. "I simply felt like celebrating."

He moved closer, his eyes still fixed on her. "You make me feel like celebrating, too, Mallory."

She could tell that he was about to take her in his arms—and she was ready for it—but a flash of something bright and white caught her eye out the kitchen window. "What?"

Logan turned in time to see the sheriff's department cruiser coming up the driveway. "Huh? Wonder who that is?"

"Maybe it's Griggs," she said hopefully. "Maybe he's got more good news for us."

"Yeah, maybe." Logan nodded. "But just in case, how about if you wait in here while I go out to see what's up?"

"Yeah…okay." Mallory felt a familiar rush of panic as she watched Logan going out to meet the car. As he strolled down the driveway, a myriad of thoughts began to race through her head. Had Sanders or Forney gotten away somehow? Escaped from jail? Were there more accomplices? Perhaps they were in danger right now and didn't even know it. The cruiser stopped, but instead of Deputy Griggs getting out it was Trent Fallows. She frowned. What was he doing out here?

She watched as Logan and Trent conversed. Judging by their expressions, there was nothing too serious going on. Except that she wasn't sure she could judge by their expressions. Logan was good at keeping a calm demeanor despite any circumstances. And Trent was impossible to read.

After a few minutes, Logan came back into the house. "What's up?" she asked, trying not to sound overly fearful.

"Nothing really. The sheriff's department just felt that they should send a deputy out here to keep an eye on things tonight."

"And they sent Trent?"

"Until midnight. Griggs will take over after that."

"But there's not really anything wrong?"

"No." He shook his head. "Just routine."

She took in a deep breath. "So we can still relax?"

"Absolutely." Logan grinned. "Should I start up the grill?"

She glanced at the kitchen clock, surprised to see it was nearly seven. "Yeah, sure. Why not?" She got the plate of seasoned chicken from the fridge and sat it on the counter, watching as the cruiser moved over to one side of the driveway, partly obscured by a clump of pines.

"I asked Trent to park out of the way," Logan told her. "So we can at least *imagine* we're not being watched."

"Thanks." Mallory frowned out the window. Was Trent really here to make sure they were safe? Or was he here because he still believed she was behind all these hideous crimes? She thought about asking Logan about this, but most of all she just wanted to put the whole thing behind them. At least for tonight. She was so ready for a break.

Mallory went to the windows that overlooked the deck out back. She watched as Logan fiddled with her dad's rusty old gas barbecue, bringing it to life. How was it that guys just intuitively knew how to do that?

She smiled to herself as she admired Logan from this angle. Such a nice profile. This guy was definitely easy to look at. She honestly didn't think she could ever get tired of that face. But what would happen to their relationship when she returned to Portland? As much as she hated to admit it, that was troubling her. A lot. Now that this thing was coming to an end—or at least she hoped it was—she got the feeling that she and Logan were coming to an end, too. It was almost as though they'd been playing a game. Or were actors in a fast-moving film…and the credits were about to roll.

As Logan put the chicken breasts on the grill, she wondered just how interested he was in her. Oh, he'd certainly appeared interested. And those kisses…well, it wouldn't be easy to say goodbye to that. But what if he'd simply been enjoying playing the role of her protector? What if he'd only stuck around to keep his promise to her dad? Or he simply liked the excitement? Even if he was looking for something more, was it the kind of something more that would last a lifetime? Or, like most guys these days, was he just looking for a temporary relationship?

"That should be ready in about twenty minutes," he said as he came back in. "But it's awfully nice out there. Want to eat outside?"

"Sounds good." She handed him the stack of plates, napkins and silverware. "Why don't you go set the table and I'll bring the other things out." As she removed the salads from the fridge, she noticed a chilled bottle of sparkling cider in the back. And although it was premature, she felt celebratory. As far as she knew, this was their first fear-free night together...perhaps their last night together, too.

"Special occasion?" Logan asked as she handed him the bottle.

"Sort of," she said. "I mean, it feels like we're out of harm's way."

His expression was hard to read as he opened the bottle. Almost as if he was worried, and she wondered if there was something he hadn't told her. Just the same, she wasn't sure she wanted to think about that right now. Even if this was fool's paradise, she wanted to linger here awhile.

"And it's probably my last night here," she said. "I promised Detective Doyle that I'd be in Portland on Monday morning. So I guess I should go back tomorrow."

"Is that safe?" He filled the glasses, handing one to her.

"I don't know. But here's to safety." She smiled as she dinged her glass against his.

"To safety," he said a bit glumly.

"When I emailed Janice Doyle today—with the news story and a list of my research sources—I told her that I wouldn't feel safe returning to my apartment unless Brock was in custody. Or unless the police provide me with a bodyguard." She made a sheepish grin. "But so far, Detective Doyle hasn't responded. But it seemed a reasonable request…in light of everything."

"Reasonable to you, anyway."

Mallory's earlier cheer was starting to wear thin. "Maybe we should talk about something else," she said quietly.

"Good idea."

And so, while the chicken was grilling, they made small talk, carefully skirting the elephant in the room. Or perhaps there were a pair of pachyderms parked there.

"This is much better than eating at a restaurant in town," Logan said as they sat down in the Adirondack chairs that Mallory's dad had made when she was a girl.

"Much better." She leaned back and breathed in a deep breath of fresh pine scented air. "I think I could get used to this."

"Get *used* to it?" Logan chuckled. "You grew up here, remember?"

She chuckled. "Yeah. But I'm a city girl now. Remember?"

"And you like that better?"

She pursed her lips. Did she?

"I mean, it's okay if you do. Lots of people can't stand rural living."

"I actually like both." She looked at the tall green trees and sighed. "And the truth is I sometimes miss this. Probably more than I like to admit." She took a sip of the cider. "And after what happened…to Kestra…well, I told myself I was never going back there."

"Uh-huh?"

"But that was probably a knee-jerk reaction."

"Seems like a pretty natural reaction to me."

"Yeah…but it's kind of like making a hair decision."

"Huh? A hair decision?"

She laughed. "Yeah, it's a girl thing. But you're never supposed to make a decision to cut your hair or change a style on a bad hair day."

"Oh...yeah, so you don't regret what you gave up."

"That's right. So, I probably shouldn't make up my mind about my future in Portland, either. Not until I'm in a better place." She shook her head. "And I'll definitely get a different apartment if I—" She stopped talking to listen—she'd heard what sounded like a twig breaking beneath a foot. "Did you hear that?"

Logan was sitting up straight now. "Yeah," he said quietly.

"Probably just a deer," she whispered, still listening.

"Yeah. Probably."

"Or maybe a cougar or a bear," she said in a teasing tone. "I hear they've been spotted around here."

"That's true." Logan squinted up at the sky. "But seems a little early in the evening for them to be on the prowl. They're pretty nocturnal, you know."

"Probably a deer." She tried to sound more confident than she felt.

Before long, the chicken was done and they moved to the table to eat. "Mind if I say a blessing?" Logan asked.

"Not at all. I'd love it."

"Dear Father in Heaven," he began. "We thank You for this food and ask Your blessing on it. We also thank You for our friendship and ask Your blessing on it, as well. Thank You for directing our paths and for keeping us safe. We are grateful. Amen."

"Amen," she echoed.

"This really is nice out here." Logan laid his napkin in his lap.

"Pretty sweet." She put a serving of salad on a plate, handed it to him.

"And the food's not bad, either." He grinned as he forked into a piece of chicken.

"And I have a suggestion." She loaded her own salad plate.

"What's that?"

"Just during dinner, let's put a moratorium on any conversation about—"

"Yes," he said quickly, "I was just thinking the same thing. *Agreed.*"

It was the loveliest meal Mallory could ever remember eating. Mostly due to the company, although the food was pretty good, too. As the sun began setting low in the sky, she wished this moment could go on forever. Everything was so perfect.

"This has been fabulous," Logan said as he laid his napkin alongside his plate.

"I was just thinking the same thing."

"But it's getting dark." He glanced over his shoulder. "And maybe I'm just suffering some form of PSTD—okay, that's an exaggeration—but I would feel better if we went inside. And I did assure Deputy Griggs that we wouldn't let our guard down."

"Yeah." She gathered up some dishes and things. "As much as I hate to go inside, I think you're right."

As Mallory started rinsing the dishes, Logan went around the house pulling the drapes and shades closed. But instead of giving into fear—which really didn't seem necessary—Mallory decided to simply enjoy being holed up in here with him.

"At least Trent won't be able to spy on us," Logan said in a teasing tone as he returned to the kitchen.

They made cheerful banter as they finished cleaning up and putting away. As Mallory gave a final wipe to the countertop, she decided that they made a good team. She wondered what it would be like to live like this always— with Logan by her side.

"You look deep in thought," Logan said.

"Oh?" She blinked. "Just daydreaming, I guess."

"You're probably tired," he told her. "All the recent excitement is pretty exhausting. I know how much I needed that long nap today."

"No…" She hung up the dishrag. "I'm not tired." She peered curiously at him, suddenly feeling guilty for how much of his weekend she'd taken. What if he had wanted to do something else? Like sleep in his own bed? "You know you don't have to stay here with me," she said suddenly. "With those two men locked up and Deputy Trent outside, I'm sure I'm safe here now."

Logan's brow creased. "What if I just feel better being around? I mean, unless you have a problem with me sleeping on the sofa."

"No, not at all. I actually feel much safer with you here." He smiled.

She pointed to the DVD cabinet by the TV. "Want to watch a movie or something? My dad has a pretty good selection of action films. Unless you prefer my mom's chick flicks." She poked him in the ribs. "Yeah, you really look like a chick-flick kinda guy."

He laughed. "You might be surprised to know that I sometimes do enjoy a quality romantic film with my mom and sister."

"That's what I like. A manly man with a feminine side. The best of both worlds." She giggled. "You can pick it out." She watched as he looked through the DVDs, finally selecting one of her all time favorite films. *"To Kill a Mockingbird!"* she exclaimed.

"Is that a problem?"

"Not at all. I love that movie. I haven't seen it for years." She hurried back to the kitchen. "This calls for popcorn."

"And ice cream," he called out.

The movie was just ending when she heard her phone chiming on the coffee table. "Maybe that's Dad," she said cheerfully. "He might've got an earlier flight." But when she picked up the phone, she saw that the text was from "unknown." "Oh, no," she gasped as she looked at the words.

"What is it?" Logan asked.

"Look." She held it out for him to see.

Enjoy your last few hours with your boyfriend. Because it ends tonight.

TWENTY-ONE

"It has to be Brock," she said somberly. "It just has to be."

"But he's in Portland," Logan reminded her. "He anchors the eleven o'clock news, right?"

"Right." She pointed to the clock above the fireplace. "It's almost eleven."

Logan grabbed the remote, turning the TV back on and tuning it to the right channel, where a car ad was playing. As much as he didn't enjoy seeing Brock Dennison's face, it would be reassuring tonight. For both of them. Because although he hated to admit it and didn't want to frighten Mallory, he felt certain that—if her theory was correct—Brock really was her biggest threat. But since Portland was three hours away and the news show ran for thirty minutes…they still had time to do something about it.

They watched in silence as the news came on. But Mallory reached for Logan's hand when they realized it was another newscaster seated beside the vivacious blonde Abby Kingston. Abby did some quick highlights then explained Brock's absence. "As many of you know, our beloved anchor has endured a difficult week," she said with compassion. "Faithfully coming into work despite his personal loss. And just today, he delivered a touching eulogy at murder victim Kestra Williams's funeral, which we'll show you some footage of later, but our generous station manager insisted Brock take some much needed time off. We'll all be glad to see him back here tomorrow evening. Now for a quick look at—" Logan turned it off.

"What do we do?" Mallory asked with fearful eyes. "What do you think this means?"

"Maybe nothing." Brock stood up, taking her hand. "And I'm probably overreacting, and I hope I'm wrong, but I'd rather err on the side of caution. Just in case. Come on." He led her down the hallway to the bear cave and, after they were securely locked in the room, did a quick inventory of the firearms and unused rounds of ammo, still displayed on the coffee table like a mini arsenal. "We just need to be prepared...for anything."

"Good call." Mallory sat down in the office chair with a perplexed expression. "There's something that's been nagging at me," she muttered. "I didn't really want to think about it anymore. But it doesn't go away."

"What's that?"

"Trent." She looked up, peering into his eyes. "I honestly don't know what to make of that guy. I mean he seemed convinced that I was still behind everything—even suspecting I was the one to sneak into the hospital and smother Perez." She scowled. "And yet he's the one who comes out here? To *protect* me? And in the back of my mind, I still hear my dad saying 'don't trust him,' but there he is parked in front of our house. Seems kinda weird."

"Yeah. I had similar thoughts."

She picked up her pistol and holster, laying it in her lap along with her cell phone—almost as if she was getting herself armed up and ready. Probably not a bad idea. "So, when does Deputy Griggs get here, anyway?"

"Soon." Logan glanced at his watch. "Well, about forty minutes."

"Good." Mallory seemed to relax a little. "I'll feel better having him around."

"I get what you mean about Trent," Logan admitted. "He's a hard one to figure out. He acts like he's dedicated to law enforcement, and yet from what I hear, he's kind of a lone ranger and most of the deputies don't really like him."

"And there's that little fact, how he just happened to go to the same college as Brock."

"Yeah." Logan nodded. "I kind of forgot that."

"What if he has a connection to Brock? What if he's actually working for him?"

Logan considered this. "I don't know, Mallory. I mean, it just seems way too convenient. Trent has been a deputy in Clover a few years now. It's not like Brock could've planted him here just to get to you. And then, if you think about it, it seems awfully convenient. I mean that Trent could really be working for Brock. You know?"

She nodded. "Yeah, I guess you're right."

"But back to Brock," Logan said slowly. "Do you know if he's familiar with firearms? Does he own any guns?"

Her eyes grew wide. "What are you saying?"

"Well, like I said, he wasn't on the news tonight…which means he could be anywhere. If Sanders and Perez really were his hit men—and they obviously messed up—well, what if Brock decided to take matters into his own hands? What if wanted to finish things up himself? But unless he's experienced with firearms, I don't think we need to feel too threatened. Do you know if he owns a gun?"

Her brow creased. "Yeah…he's really into duck hunting, and he's got a pretty impressive shotgun collection. And he goes out skeet shooting quite a bit. He took me once. He's a good shot."

"Oh…" Logan didn't like the sound of this. "Okay. Good to know."

Mallory stood up, frowning at her rumpled sundress. "I'd really like to get into my jeans now. Is it okay if I go upstairs to my room?"

"Good idea. I'll stay nearby and keep an eye on things."

"Thanks." She picked up her holster and phone and headed back down the darkened hallway with him trailing her. "It'll just take a minute or two," she quietly told him.

"I'll be right here." Feeling somewhat like a sentry, but suddenly wondering why he hadn't strapped on the Ruger holster, he stood at the foot of the stairs waiting. Still, he told himself, he'd probably overreacted. Just because Brock had been MIA on the news was no reason to go off the deep end. And to go prowling around a darkened house with firearms probably wasn't terribly prudent. Just as he decided to tell Mallory, he heard a loud boom outside in the yard.

It was definitely a gunshot; it sounded like a large rifle or even a shotgun. And suddenly he remembered what Mallory had said about Brock's guns. Hunching down, he was headed for the bear cave to grab a firearm when he heard another loud boom.

"Stay put," he yelled up the stairs as he ran through the house with the AR rifle and a box of rounds that he shoved in his pocket.

"What happened?" she screamed. "Are you okay?"

"Yeah," he yelled back. "But you stay put—and call for help!" Leaning against the wall between the door jamb and the window, he peered outside. Fortunately the exterior lights were on and it wasn't difficult to see the yard around the house. But there was no movement. *Nothing.*

Mallory had barely pulled on her jeans when she heard the first gunshot. Logan had commanded her to remain upstairs, so she threw on her flannel shirt over the sundress, and she was just shoving her feet into her hiking shoes when she heard the second blast. Feeling seriously alarmed, she strapped on her holster and wished she'd thought to grab a box of ammo, too. But at least it was loaded. Now all she could do was wait.

And, instead of running down there as she wanted to do, she reached for her phone, but afraid to make any noise in case someone was in the house, she put it on quiet mode and texted Deputy Griggs. Help. Gunshots. Help. She shot up a quick silent prayer as she hit Send. *Please protect Logan. Get help here fast. Please!*

Despite Logan's orders to stay put, she was ready to burst downstairs and help him. But she remembered their agreement—he was calling the shots. It was possible he knew something she didn't. Perhaps the shooter was in the house. And although she couldn't lock her door, she could keep quiet…and wait. Plus she had her gun. But as each second dragged by, her patience was wearing thin. What was going on?

She was just about to go peek down the staircase when she heard the sound of quiet footsteps downstairs. Was that Logan? Should she call out? But what if she put him in danger? Better to just lie low…wait it out. And pray. It seemed as if an hour went by, but according to her phone it was less than four minutes when another loud boom, followed by the sound of breaking glass, broke the silence. Followed by nothing but more silence. What was going on?

The silence was so thick and deep that Logan almost wondered if he'd imagined those gunshots. But as he peeked through the crack in the front room drapes, he caught sight of the cruiser's fluorescent strips glowing from the garage light. The car was still parked behind the trees, but unless he was mistaken, the driver's door was opened. Had Trent fired those shots? And if so, why?

Suddenly he saw what looked like Trent's uniform. He was down on the ground just a few feet from his vehicle. At first Logan thought perhaps Trent was on his belly in order to get off a good shot without making himself into an easy target, but then he noticed that Trent appeared to be struggling, trying to crawl. As if he'd been shot.

With no time to think or reason, Logan ran through the house, exited through the laundry room into the garage and slipped out the side door of the garage. Hanging in the shadows while his eyes adjusted to the darkness, he hunkered down and sprinted toward Trent. Grabbing him by the arms, Logan dragged him the short distance to the garage. Two more shots rang in his ears.

"Can you walk?" he asked Trent as he locked the door behind him. From what he'd seen in the exterior light, Trent had been shot in the chest and face. But based on distance between his shotgun wounds, the shooter hadn't been too close. If Trent was blessed, the shots weren't life threatening. But he was still a mess.

"Don't know," Trent huffed.

Another loud shot rang out, followed by the sound of breaking glass. Logan grabbed up what looked like a drop cloth and tossed it over the wounded deputy to completely cover him. "Keep quiet and maybe you'll be okay. Gotta help Mallory. She was calling the cops." Logan crept into the house, where he saw the front window had been shattered by a gunshot. He paused to listen, but hearing nothing, headed for the bear cave to get his cell phone, then doubled back to find Mallory. They had to get out of here—*fast*.

Halfway down the hallway, he noticed something directly ahead that made his blood run cold. Standing in front of the broken window, illuminated by the porch light, a tall man faced Logan. Wearing a black ski mask and gloves, he was dressed from head to toe in dark camouflage, aiming what appeared to be a semiautomatic shotgun straight at Logan.

Hoping that he was still somewhat concealed in the hallway shadows, Logan froze in place. Without breathing, he

slowly raised the AR rifle, ready to shoot. "Drop it or—"
Before he could finish, his ears rang with a loud boom and
he tumbled back into a wall. Before he hit the ground, he
returned the shot, then crawled into the master bedroom
doorway for cover.

"Get out of here!" Logan yelled at the top of his lungs.
He wasn't talking to the shooter—although he hoped the
monster would think so—but his instructions were for Mallory. "Get out *now*!" he hollered as he closed and locked
the door. *Run for your life, Mallory.*

Logan clutched his left shoulder where the shotgun had
clipped him. It was wet with blood and burned like fire,
but the shooter's aim had been off. Otherwise Logan would
be dead. He heard footsteps down the hallway and figured the creep was coming to finish him off. Hurrying
into the bathroom, he locked the door and bundled a bath
towel around his bleeding shoulder. He was just reaching
for his phone when he heard a loud crash that seemed to
come from upstairs.

"Mallory!" he gasped. Had the intruder gone up there
and kicked her door in? Had he found her? Armed with
the AR, Logan crept through the bedroom—listening intently at the door, he slowly opened it. His goal: to save
Mallory—or die trying.

TWENTY-TWO

Frozen in fear, Mallory tried to think. Logan had told her to run—but where was she supposed to go? She'd heard the shots, knew an intruder was in the house. If she went downstairs she'd probably run straight into him. But maybe that would be a good thing. If she was prepared, she might be able to shoot him. And it was possible that Logan needed her backup. And yet she had promised to do as he said— and he had said to run. *But where?*

Suddenly she remembered the way she and Austin had sometimes sneaked out of the second floor when they were kids. Austin had discovered how, revealing it to her when she was a young teen. She hadn't attempted it for ages. She tiptoed to the nearby bathroom and quietly slid open the window, looking down onto the wooden pergola below. This pine structure had been there for as long as she could remember. It shaded a small courtyard outside of her parents' bathroom—her mom's secret sunbathing spot. Mallory prayed that the old wooden structure was still strong enough to support her weight as she eased herself out the window. She also hoped that she could still do a balance-beam walk, as she attempted to traverse the narrow piece of wood. She was nearly to the edge—everything intact— when she felt the whole thing swaying. And suddenly it was giving way and all she could do was to take a flying leap and hope she landed in the soft grass without breaking any bones.

As she heard the pergola crashing down behind her, she leaped to her feet and took off sprinting across the lawn, making a beeline for the safety of the darkened woods. When she left the soft grassy area, her footsteps grew loud. Pinecones and needles crunched beneath her hiking shoes as she ran through the underbrush, dodging the trees, trying to stay in the shadows. She knew she'd just given herself away with the fallen pergola, and the only escape was the trees, but she needed to get deep into the woods fast. Her best hope was to find a safe spot and wait for Logan. If only he was okay.

She didn't know how far she'd gone when she finally stopped next to a thicket of pines, but she was panting hard and her sides ached from running. Holding her breath to listen for the sound of footsteps coming up behind her, she counted to ten and was relieved to hear only silence. She slowly exhaled and inhaled through her mouth, trying to remain quiet while she attempted to catch her breath… watching for the beam of a flashlight…and waiting. She felt reasonably safe, but all she could think of was Logan. *Where was he? Was he okay?*

If he was okay, would he know to come out here to find her? If he wasn't okay…? She couldn't think about that. It was too much to bear. Instead, she shot up another silent prayer. *Please, God—protect him!*

She pulled out her phone again, checking to see if Griggs had responded to her text—if help was on the way. But realizing that her phone had not had bars while in the house, she sent it again. She considered texting Logan, too—to see if he was okay. But if he was still in the house, possibly hiding in her dad's office, and hadn't thought to silence his phone, a chiming noise would put him in harm's way.

Mallory listened hard but heard nothing. Even the woods

were unnaturally silent, as if the wildlife was holding its breath, too. The only thing she could hear was Logan's last words to her. His warning kept reverberating in her ears. *Get out. Run. Now.* He'd obviously been in serious danger and wanted her to escape it. But now what? How long could she stay out here without going back to help him? Again she prayed, this time it was for God's direction—*Show me what to do—please!* But nothing came to her. Nothing besides questions. Too many questions.

What if...what if? Every horrible scenario was racing through her mind now. Anything and everything seemed possible. And if something bad happened to Logan she would blame herself. She reached down to touch the pistol in her holster again. Just six bullets. Not a lot, but enough to make a difference. Enough to possibly save his life. And he wasn't out here to tell her what to do. Maybe it was time to do it her way.

She peered back at the house. Even though it wasn't close, the exterior lights showed up clearly through the trees. As far as she could see, no one was outside. She stepped out into the open, ready to go back, to sneak inside, and help Logan. But then she remembered her promise to let him be the chief. He was supposed to call the shots. And he had told her to run—in no uncertain terms. But what now?

And surely the rules would change if something happened to him? What if he was no longer able to call the shots? What if he needed her? How would she know out here in the woods? Sure, she might be safe...but what about him?

Logan, her heart whispered, *please be safe—be okay. I need you.*

Another gunshot made her skin crawl. Who was doing the shooting? What was going on? And where was Logan? Furthermore, where was Griggs? And the backup? And what about Trent? She pulled her phone out of her jeans pocket, cupping her hand to shield the light so it wouldn't expose her presence in the pitch-black woods, she peered down to see that Griggs had finally received her text and texted her back. On my way with backup. Five minutes out. Where are you?

She texted back. In the woods. Logan in house. Shooter in house.

He texted again. Trent?

She frowned as she texted back. Don't know. As she hit Send, she wondered if Trent could possibly be the shooter. But as Logan had said earlier, that didn't make any sense. As much as she distrusted Trent, she didn't think he was part of Brock's diabolical plan. He would have too much to lose.

And although she hadn't seen Brock and had no real proof, she could just feel it deep inside of her. He was here. And he was here to kill her…and anyone else who got in his way.

Oh, she knew people thought she was crazy and that no one besides Logan could believe that the smooth-talking news anchor was really a murderer. But she felt certain that Brock was the shooter tonight. And this is just what she texted Griggs.

I suspect Brock Dennison is on the property. Armed with shotgun.

A chill ran through her as she hit Send. If she and Logan didn't survive this night, and if Brock got away somehow, at least she would have shared that important piece of information. At least law enforcement could go after him later. If it wasn't him…well, she couldn't even find an answer for that.

She stared at the house, wondering how long she could

stay back here with the possibility that Logan's life was in peril. She ran her hand over the gun's handle and honestly thought she could feel her finger itching. If Brock was in there, if he had hurt Logan, well, she would rather die trying to take down Brock than to survive out here and lose Logan. Suddenly her decision was clear.

"Forgive me, Logan," she whispered as she headed purposefully toward the house. As she slowly walked, trying to keep her footsteps as quiet as possible, she slipped the pistol from the holster and readied it to shoot. She knew that her old-fashioned single-action pistol was no match for what Brock might be packing, but a well-placed bullet *could* help Logan escape.

She was nearly at the lawn area when she felt her phone vibrating in her pocket. Ducking behind the thick trunk of a pine, she shielded the light with her hand and peered down to read the text message. The first thing she saw was that it was from "unknown."

If you want to see your boyfriend again, come back. Now.

She blinked down at the words. No veiled threats here. Brock was playing hardball. And it was in his court.

I don't believe you, she boldly texted back, just trying to buy time…to think.

Then he's a dead duck.

She knew she had to get the upper hand here. But how? She decided to try again. If Logan's with you, she typed with trembling thumbs, have him text me from his phone. There was a longer pause this time. So long she felt worried. But eventually another text popped up. To her relief it was sent from Logan's phone. Obey the chief was all it said. But at least she knew it was from him. Brock wouldn't write that.

And she knew Logan was warning her to stay away—just as much as she knew that was impossible.

Will do, she texted back. But even as she sent it, she knew she wouldn't. Brock obviously had Logan. And he obviously planned to kill him. Just as he'd killed Kestra and planned to kill Mallory. Brock was a madman who believed he could get away with murder. Indeed, he had gotten away with it.

But what should she do? How could she handle this without endangering Logan or herself even more? She knew backup would be here soon. But with Brock holding Logan in the house…and if she joined them…backup would become more difficult. Instead of needing to rescue one person, they might have to rescue two. Complications. And so she decided to text Brock again. She had to gain some control. Meet me out back, she texted. Unless I see Logan, I won't reveal myself.

Brock quickly responded. On our way out. No tricks or Logan gets it.

No tricks, she texted back. But that wasn't a promise. It was a warning…to him. She remained behind the trunk of the large pine, practicing her aim, with her gun ready to shoot. Taking some deep breaths, she knew she had to get calm. *Don't shoot until ready.* And once she shot, she would have to take cover fast.

Because once she shot, the rules would change. If she missed him, Brock might retaliate by killing Logan. Even if he returned fire at her, she would only have five more shots to take him out and it would be crazy by then. What if she accidentally shot Logan? So, really, it depended on one good shot. Unless her aim was true, Brock would have all the advantages—and the ammo.

Praying for a cool head and a steady hand, she waited. Watching as the exterior lights were turned out. Of course, Brock was trying to hide in the darkness. She closed her eyes for a moment, trying to adjust her vision to blackness. When she looked back at the darkened house, she was surprised that she was able to see its outline as well as the night sky reflecting on the sliding glass doors. If Brock exited onto the back deck, she might be able to see him. And then she heard the lock on the sliding door being unlocked.

Ducking back behind the tree trunk and shielding her phone beneath her shirt, she sent a quick text to Griggs. Backyard. Brock has Logan. Exiting back door—

She didn't finish the text because she heard the slider door opening. She hit Send, tucked her phone in her jeans pocket and peered out from behind the tree.

She could see the two of them like one big, bulky shadow. One was slightly slumped over. But the other one, despite his dark disguise, she recognized as Brock. Of course he was using Logan as his shield. Even if she was an excellent shot, which was a stretch, it seemed impossible to get to Brock without hitting Logan. What now?

"Stay hidden!" Logan yelled. Then Brock swore angrily, hitting Logan so hard she could hear the smack clear across the yard.

She was tempted to scream something back, but knew that would give her hiding spot away. Instead, she decided to text Brock again. From behind the tree, she held her phone under her shirt as she hurried to type. Let Logan go, and I'll step out. I promise.

She looked out again, trying to see if Brock was going to check his phone. "Don't bother trying to text me now, Mallory. I won't fall for it," he yelled. "Just get yourself out here before I shoot your boyfriend *again*."

So he'd already shot Logan? Mallory's heart clenched. How bad was it? She played out a scenario in her mind— if she just randomly shot into the air, would Brock be distracted enough to loosen his grip on Logan? Perhaps Logan could make a run for it? Or would Brock simply shoot Logan then aim at her?

"Let Logan go," she yelled impulsively. "And you can have *me*."

Brock turned in the direction of her voice, aiming into the woods, but obviously uncertain because he didn't shoot.

"Come on," she yelled from behind the tree trunk. "You let Logan go and I'll step out, Brock."

This time his answer came in the loud boom of the shotgun that seemed to splatter all around her. She answered him with a shot from her rifle, not aiming at Brock and Logan, but into the woods in the hope it would distract Brock and buy her some time. She was about to shoot again when she heard another shot—not the big boom of a shotgun, but the clear, loud ring of a rifle.

In the same instant she heard men's voices yelling, and she peeked out from the tree trunk in time to see Brock and Logan tumbling to the ground. It suddenly looked like a dog pile with several other men in deputy uniforms jumping on top, a scrambling heap of arms and legs. She held her breath, waiting, and was thankful that no more shots were fired.

With her gun still ready to shoot, she hurried over to the scene just as Deputies Griggs and O'Brian pinned Brock facedown in the grass. From the beam of a deputy flashlight, she could see Brock was dressed in his duck-hunting camouflage. But seeing him down there, spread-eagled, as they frisked then handcuffed him, with a dark splotch of blood growing on his side, she knew he wasn't going anywhere.

While Griggs was talking on the radio to the other backup deputies in law enforcement code, she holstered her gun and went to where Logan was sitting on the grass, his elbows on his knees, with a slightly dazed expression.

She knelt down beside him, throwing her arms around him in relief.

"Are you okay?" she asked quietly, trying not to stare at the shoulder that had been shot.

"I am now." He gave her a crooked smile. "Nice work, Mallory."

"Medical care should be here any minute," Griggs called out as they rolled Brock over, forcing him to sit up. Griggs reached over to jerk the black ski mask off his head, shining the bright flashlight into his face. "Well, I'll be," Griggs declared. "If it ain't that fancy-dancy Portland anchorman—Brock Dennison."

"You gotta be kidding." O'Brian leaned down to stare hard, shaking his head in clear disbelief.

"You were right after all, Mallory," Griggs hollered over his shoulder. "I'm sure Portland PD will be glad to know we got their killer."

As more low enforcement flocked into the backyard, Logan told Griggs about Trent. "He's in the garage, under a tarp by the side door. Shot bad. Needs medical care."

"So do you." Mallory put her hand on Logan's good shoulder as he attempted to stand. "Why not just wait here," she suggested. "Let your EMTs take care of you for a change."

He sighed, leaning into her. "Good idea."

As Mallory drove her car behind the ambulances to the hospital, she pulled out her Bluetooth to call her dad. "I'm sorry to wake you," she said when he answered in a groggy voice.

"What's wrong?" he demanded, "Are you okay?"

"Yes, I'm fine." And she gave him the whole lowdown and, although she could tell he was relieved, he also sounded slightly disappointed not to have been there, to have missed out on all the action. "Well, I'm just glad you're okay, sweetie," he finally said. "I was kicking myself for giving up that standby tonight. I drove a rental car back to back to Iowa, but all the way there, I felt like I'd made a mistake. Like I should've come, anyway."

"I'm glad you're back with Mom," she said. "I love you both and I hope you enjoy the rest of your trip." She chuckled as she pulled up at the hospital. "And I promise to get your house back into shape before you get home. Might take a while."

"Don't worry about that for now. Just go give the fire chief a big hug and tell him thanks for me."

"For sure," she said as she got out of the car.

"I told you Logan McDaniel was a good man," he said.

"You were right, Dad." She smiled to herself as she went into the hospital lobby. Logan was a good man. A really good man. And despite the horrifying nightmare she'd been through, she knew she never would've gotten to know Logan the way she'd done without it. The big question now was…where did they go from here? They obviously had two very different lives in two different places. Was this amazing interlude with Logan about to end? And, if so, was she willing to let it?

TWENTY-THREE

Logan hadn't seen Trent Fallows since dragging him into the Myerses' garage last night. But as he walked down to Trent's room the following morning, he knew that he'd fared much better than Deputy Fallows. Mallory had assured him of as much last night before she'd gone home.

"According to Griggs, Trent lost a lot of blood," she'd quietly explained. "He was in bad shape when they brought him in."

"That's too bad."

"Well, he might've died if you hadn't covered him like that," she said. "Griggs said he was in shock when they found him. Besides hiding him from Brock, that tarp helped to keep him warm."

"Well, I hope he'll be okay." And Logan had meant it. In some ways, despite Trent's obnoxious ways, his presence at the house last night might've helped to save Mallory's and Logan's lives. And Logan intended to thank him for it—for both of them.

"Hey, Trent," Logan said in a friendly tone as he entered the room. "It's Logan." Trent's entire head, including his eyes, was bandaged, as was much of his upper body. "You look like a mess, man."

"Yeah…pretty much," Trent mumbled. "Heard you got shot, too."

"Not nearly as bad as you." Logan touched the bandage on his shoulder.

"Guess I was wrong about Brock Dennison," Trent said quietly.

"A lot of folks were." Logan sat next to him. "And I can admit now that I even had my doubts a few times. A big newsman like Brock Dennison just didn't seem like a real likely murder suspect."

"O'Brian was by," Trent said slowly. "They got a full confession out of Dennison."

"Hard to say you're innocent when you get caught red-handed."

"Yeah...what a mess."

"So, anyway, Trent, I came by to thank you for being out at the Myerses' place last night. It occurred to me this morning that your presence might've made the difference between life and death for Mallory and me. On behalf of both of us, I want to thank you."

Trent didn't say anything.

"And I'm sorry you got shot so bad," Logan continued.

"That was my own fault," Trent muttered. "Let my guard down."

"So did we," Logan told him. "Brock took us all by surprise."

"I'm glad they got him." Trent was clenching and unclenching his fists. "I've been thinking a lot about the girl in college...Amanda Samuels...Brock's girlfriend that went missing. Real pretty girl. And real nice. I feel certain Brock killed her, too. I told O'Brian about it."

Logan just sighed.

"Griggs said they'll question him about that."

"That'll be good."

"Guess it goes to show that you really can't judge a book by its cover. Brock was always so smooth... I just never guessed what was beneath."

"Hey, Trent," a friendly female voice spoke up. "Is this where the party is?"

Logan looked over to see Winnie and Mallory coming into the room. He greeted them both so that Trent would know who had entered.

"I just wanted to come say hello to my favorite deputy." Winnie went right to Trent's bedside, taking his hand. "And I found Mallory wandering aimlessly down the hallway." She chuckled. "Looking like a lost soul."

Mallory looked sweetly sheepish. "Well, I went to Logan's room…found his bed empty… I, uh, got a little worried…you know?"

Logan went over to Mallory, looping his good arm around her shoulder. "I was just checking on Trent. Thanking him for being there last night."

"I want to thank you, too," Mallory told him. "You put yourself in the line of fire for us, Trent. I really appreciate it. And sorry about your injuries."

"Sorry I didn't believe you, Mallory. My mistake."

"We all make mistakes," Logan said somberly. "Fortunately you can learn from this one, Trent."

"Yeah," Winnie agreed. "From what I heard, you could've been dead."

"We better go…let you rest." Logan reached over to grasp Trent's knee. "Get well, buddy."

"Yeah," Mallory said. "I've been praying for you."

Trent muttered thanks, and Logan and Mallory made a quick exit, leaving Winnie there to keep Trent company.

"Wow." Mallory shook her head as they went into Logan's room. "He looks pretty bad off, huh?"

"At least he's alive."

"So, how are you this morning?" Mallory asked brightly.

"Getting ready to check out of this place." He sat down on the edge of the bed. "Go home and get some actual rest."

"Yeah, you must be exhausted."

"How about you?" he asked. "Did you really go back to your parents' last night like you said you'd do?"

"Yep. Started cleaning the place up. Swept up the glass. Cleaned up most of the blood. Griggs has got a glass guy coming in to fix the window tomorrow. And I'll call a janitorial service to go over the whole place before my parents get back."

"You're still going to Portland today?"

"I have to go. I promised Detective Doyle I'd be there on Monday."

"Even though they've got Brock in custody? I hear they're getting a full confession."

"Yeah, Griggs told me about that." She shook her head. "Even though I knew it was true—at least, I thought it was true—it's still hard to believe." She sighed. "It's a pretty big story."

"Is that why you're going back to Portland?" Logan asked. "To return to work, to write this big story?"

She frowned. "Well, I need to take care of things. Talk to the police. Check in with the news station. Figure out my apartment. Visit Kestra's parents…her grave."

"Yeah." He looked toward the door where an elderly man was slowly moving a walker down the hallway with what appeared to be his wife by his side. There was a long pause now. Neither of them spoke. But everything in Logan wanted to beg her to forget about Portland, to just stay here, to continue this amazing relationship. But he knew that was selfish. He knew how much she'd loved her newswriting job, living in the city. How could he ask her to leave all that?

"I know we've only spent a few days together," she said quietly. "But I'm really going to miss you."

He nodded. "Yeah. Me, too."

"I wish you could come with me," she murmured.

"Come with you?" He studied her carefully. "You mean leave Clover? Give up my job? Everything?"

She looked surprised. "No. Of course not. I mean just go to Portland with me. While I get stuff figured out."

He felt a wave of relief. "Well, I am going to be off work for at least a week. How about I go to Portland with you? Help you get things straightened out."

She brightened. "Really? You'd do that?"

He smiled at her. "Oh, Mallory, don't you know by now that I'd go to the ends of the earth for you?"

She laughed. "You mean as long as it didn't involve leaving Clover or your job?"

He got serious now. "Truth is, I would probably give that all up, too. But it wouldn't be easy."

Her eyes lit up. "Really?" She stood now, coming over to stand closer to him. "Do you mean that?"

"Mallory, I've been holding back, telling myself that it's too soon—too much, too fast—but the truth is, I love you. I've known it almost since that night when I tackled you in the mud."

She placed her hand on his cheek. "Really? Well, did you know that I love you, too?" she asked.

"You do?"

She nodded shyly. "I've known it for a while."

He stood and gathered her into his arms. Kissing her with all the passion he'd been holding back since yesterday, back when he'd nearly given up on them being together. And she returned the kiss with just as much passion—until they both stepped away and just looked at each other. Mallory was wide-eyed and breathless, but she was smiling happily.

"Mallory," he said slowly. "I know this might be premature…maybe I'm jumping the gun. But we had so many close calls, so many times I thought I could lose you…and then my fear that you were leaving for good. You asked me if I would go to Portland with you… Now I want to know if you would stay in Clover for me."

"What do you mean?" She kept her eyes locked on his. "What are you saying?"

"I'm saying *I love you*, Mallory. I want to marry you. I want us to spend the rest of our lives together." He waited hopefully. "What do you say?"

She seemed to study him carefully, but without saying a word. He suddenly wondered if he'd blown it completely. "And forget what I said about staying in Clover," he said quickly. "If you want, we can live in Portland—or anywhere—as long as we're together."

"As a matter of fact, I've been rethinking living in the big city, Logan. I'm just not sure I can do that anymore."

"Well, you don't have to decide about *that* today." He reached for her hand. "But I'll repeat my question. Mallory Myers, will you marry me?"

She broke into a big smile. "Yes!" She threw her arms around him. "Yes, yes and yes!"

* * * * *

Dear Reader,

Thank you for your willingness to go on this new journey with me. Or maybe you weren't aware that *Perfect Alibi* was my first venture into writing romantic suspense. Admittedly, I wasn't sure if I was cut out for this genre at first, but as soon as I dipped my toe into the waters, I was eager to jump in. And I totally enjoyed the entire process—and even plan to create more stories like this!

My first clue that I might fit into the world of romantic suspense was my longtime love of Alfred Hitchcock stories. Also, I've always enjoyed writing stories with some elements of mystery. And, being a bit of a romantic at heart, love stories seem to come fairly naturally to me. Anyway, I hope you enjoyed the story and I hope you'll be game to read the one I'm working on now.

To learn more about me or the other books I've written (more than 200) stop by my website, www.melodycarlson.com. Or you can drop me a note at melodycarlsonbooks@gmail.com. Or say "hey" on my author page on Facebook.

Thanks Again,
Melody Carlson

COMING NEXT MONTH FROM
Love Inspired® Suspense

Available November 3, 2015

CAPITOL K-9 UNIT CHRISTMAS
Capitol K-9 Unit • by Shirlee McCoy & Lenora Worth
When danger strikes at Christmastime, two members of the
Capitol K-9 Unit meet their perfect matches in two exciting
brand-new novellas.

MURDER UNDER THE MISTLETOE
Northern Border Patrol • by Terri Reed
When single mom Heather Larson-Randall returns to her
family's Christmas tree farm in the wake of her brother's
sudden death, she finds herself in the middle of a drug
investigation. Can DEA agent Tyler Griffin keep her alive as
he tries to draw out her brother's killer?

HIGH-CALIBER HOLIDAY
First Responders • by Susan Sleeman
A trained sniper, Brady Owens keeps everyone at a distance.
But when his actions put Morgan Thorsby at risk, he owes her
his protection from the stalker who doesn't want her to survive
this Christmas.

DANGEROUS TIDINGS
Pacific Coast Private Eyes • by Dana Mentink
Donna Gallagher and Brent Mitchell's worlds collide when her
father is killed while investigating Brent's missing sister. Will
the newly minted PI and the Coast Guardsman find his sister
before it's too late?

CHRISTMAS BLACKOUT • by Maggie K. Black
Someone is searching for something on Piper Lawrence's
property this holiday season, and they'll stop at nothing to get
what they want. She'll have to rely on Benjamin Duff and his
trusty dog in order to stay alive to see Christmas.

YULETIDE ABDUCTION
Rangers Under Fire • by Virginia Vaughan
Will FBI agent Elise Richardson find Josh Adams's missing
niece in time for Christmas? Or will getting too close to the
case—and Josh—put Elise directly in the path of danger?

LISCNM1015

Morgan came to a sudden stop. Brady couldn't react fast enough to keep from bumping into her. He shot an arm around her waist to stop her from taking a nosedive. The glass fell from her hand, bouncing across the carpet but not breaking. He expected her to push free, but she clamped a hand over her mouth and pointed at the desk.

Brady followed the direction of her finger and found three red roses and another picture lying on her pristine desk.

"Not again." Brady's arm instinctively tightened around her.

She tried to swivel out of his arms but he was holding her too tight. He relaxed his grip just enough to allow her to turn, but he couldn't make himself completely let go.

"Who could be doing this?" She lifted her stricken gaze to his.

"Don't worry. We'll find out," he said, but he had no reason at this point to believe they would.

"I'm so thankful for your help." A tremulous smile found her lips.

Hoping to put her at ease, he smiled back at her.

She suddenly seemed to notice he was holding her, and she pushed against his chest to free herself. The warmth of her touch sent his senses firing and his pulse racing. He didn't want to let go, but short of making a fool of himself, he had no other choice but to release her.

After dropping her bags on the desk, she reached for the picture.

"Don't touch it," he warned.

She snapped her hand back and bent closer to look. She suddenly gasped and lurched back. "He was in my room. Oh, no. No, no, no."

Knowing he wasn't going to like what he saw, Brady stepped closer. The picture was taken of Morgan from above. The shadow of the man taking the picture fell over her as she was peacefully sleeping in her bed. Superimposed on the bottom of the picture in bright red letters were the words *We'll soon be together forever, my love*.

Don't miss
HIGH-CALIBER HOLIDAY
by Susan Sleeman,
available November 2015 wherever
Love Inspired® Suspense books and ebooks are sold.